Bloody September

A JOAN KAHN BOOK

Books by C. A. Haddad

Bloody September
The Moroccan

★ ★ ★ Bloody September

C. A. Haddad ★ ★ ★

HARPER & ROW, PUBLISHERS
NEW YORK, HAGERSTOWN, SAN FRANCISCO, LONDON

A Harper Novel of Intrigue

FIRST EDITION

Designed by Gloria Adelson

Library of Congress Cataloging in Publication Data

Haddad, C A
    Bloody September.
    I. Title.
PZ4.H126Bl   [PS3558.A3117]   813'.5'4   76–5541
ISBN 0–06–011709–5

76 77 78 79 10 9 8 7 6 5 4 3 2 1

לזכר
אהרון דלל ז״ל

★ I ★
Israel

To: Haim Zion, Minister of Defense
         Eli Lazar, Chief, Section 1–4, Shin Bet
From: Agent L-7
Subject: David Haham
Date: Month of Nisan

Subject spent relatively quiet month. No trips abroad; no suspicious visitors.

Broke off with mistress of one year. Argument over apartment. Mistress told Agent L-19 that she wanted larger apartment. Haham told mistress she wasn't worth it. Suspect possible anger against mother figure. Mistress gained twenty pounds in the year of their liaison.

Subject attended many parties given by prominent political leaders. Overly friendly to A, a leader of Likud. Could it be he's cozying up to A for possible place on election list, or is it guilt over laying A's wife?

Financial activities remain difficult to follow. Continues to transfer money outside Israel to foreign subsidiaries. Probable tax evasion.

Subject continues to adhere to his community-action program for the poor. Office still open on Wednesdays for those having problems with the government. Could be a sign of subject's latent communism or perhaps aggression against father figure—i.e., the government.

Conclusions: No sign of subject's being a threat to the state, as usual. Personality distortions considerable, as usual.

How long do I have to watch subject? It's been three years.

To: Agent L-7
From: Haim Zion, Minister of Defense
Subject: David Haham

Thanks again for your invaluable report.

                           Haim Zion, Minister of Defense

Note to Eli (tear off)
  Who is this nudnik?
        Haim

Chapter 1

MY NAME IS DAVID HAHAM, David the Wise; known to my friends as David the King; known to the world at large as David the Rich.

I would not have you believe that I have always been wise, rich and kingly. I too am mortal. Not having always been insulated by my position of eminence on the Israeli economic scene, life has been hard, depressing and embarrassing even for me; though you would never know it to look at me now. A perfumed peacock, you are thinking. (Perhaps you have seen my picture in the paper?) But that is not exactly correct. Though I do take a bath every day. But I imagine if you walked into my office, you would be immediately struck by the magnificence of my person. My hair, a tousled curly black, neatly crowns a figure kept trim by daily workouts. My suits tailored to perfection, indented to emphasize the trimness of my waist, my pants pulled tightly across my well-hung crotch and tucked softly around my smashing buttocks. After all, in middle age I must emphasize my best physical features, no longer having the advantages of easy youth. But no fabric can outline the convolutions of my mind. So you see, it is true: the outward trappings of virility and strength could hide a weak, simpering, wretched personality.

Could. But they don't. I am in truth a pillar. Of course, like everybody else, I have matured. Though I have never been— as Shakespeare would put it—a callow youth. (I just threw that in so you would know also that I am well read.) Like the people of Israel, my story is one of wanderings, turmoil, oppression and ultimate triumph.

It all started for me when I was twelve years old, returning to my house from religious school. This was in Basra, Iraq, in 1948. My father, a wealthy merchant, operated an import-export firm out of Basra, a port city. We lived in a charming villa with maids, chauffeur, bougainvillaea. My mother was a beautiful woman with soft olive skin. I was her eldest. Younger than I was Amalia, a sweet little ten-year-old, and Joshua, my baby brother, aged five. Though there was much talk about the new state of Israel at that time, both in my family and in Iraq as a whole, I was only romantically affected by it. It was a dangerous time, my father had told me. Be careful how you walk; be careful how you act; be careful what you say. But we were Jews in a hostile Arab world. We had learned to be careful from the day of our circumcision.

I expected no trouble. But that is the moment when trouble waits. I returned home from school, midrash in hand, to find my family dead and our villa plundered. My father was up against a palm tree with his throat slit. Amalia's eyes were open. Her clothes were torn. She had been raped; a knife stuck up from the middle of her heart. My mother was just outside the doorway, clutching Joshua to her. She also had been raped. Joshua must have tried to interfere. He was lying across her with a knife in his back. I leaned down to smooth my mother's hair. She had always kept it in a neat bun and it disturbed me to see it out of place. She flickered her eyes. My heart jumped at the thought of her being alive.

"David," she whispered to me, "you must leave this place before they kill you too. Take the star from around my neck. It is a sign of this house. Go to your father's brother in Israel, in Beersheba. You are my first-born, your father's seed. You must survive. Remember us in Zion."

And so she died, caressing me with her eyes.

But I could not leave my family, not like that. They must be buried. I went to my neighbors and asked for help, but no one would come. They were afraid. The Arabs would be back. It was said that the chief of police had marked the villa down as his own. Through the hours, I worked alone to dig a grave deep enough for all. By evening it was done. I lowered my family into the earth and said Kaddish. Then I looked up into the heavens and cursed the God of Abraham. He paid no attention.

Now that my life in Basra was over, I was in a rush to leave. I packed a little water and some food and set out toward Israel. By that time my insanity was such that I went the wrong way. To escape from Iraq I had merely to slip across the border into Iran and contact a Jewish Agency official there. But to a child, direction is a straight line, and the straightest line to Israel was across Iraq through Jordan and into the Promised Land. It was this overland route that I took.

I consider the time I spent traveling through Arab lands very valuable. It gave me a familiarity with the land and the people that would prove useful in the years to come. Of course I had no trouble passing as an Arab. I looked like an Arab; I spoke like an Arab. And I was a mere boy, so easily overlooked by those who were watching.

Making it to Israel three months after I left Basra, I remember not knowing which territory was in Arab hands and which territory was in Jewish hands, so I went all the way to Tel Aviv to make sure. I told my story to an off-duty policeman I found in a coffee shop. He was big and blond and could barely understand my Biblical Hebrew, or was it my accent or pronunciation? Or was he just not interested?

"Don't I have enough trouble!" he shouted to the world at large as he grabbed me by my upper arm and dragged me off to some official who sent me to another official who sent me to another official who sent me to a camp. The camp was in the desert. It was filled with other immigrants like me, those from other Arab countries besides Iraq. Every family at this camp had a tent. No one knew what to do with me as I had no family. The agency officials spent a lot of time trying to find a family to take me in but the tents were small and the families large. Finally a family from Algeria let me spend the night. I gave them my food ration. Their child was tubercular.

When I was finally processed by the Jewish Agency and about to be sent to a children's kibbutz, I mentioned Uncle Elias in Beersheba, my father's brother. Uncle Elias came for me the next week.

If I were to call Uncle Elias a sadistic brute, it would be an understatement. He had two children, a boy my age and a daughter a year younger. I was overjoyed at the prospect of being a member of a family again. But it was not to be. Uncle Elias made sure right from the beginning that I knew I was a charity case and not their equal. I took to comparing his attitude with that of my father, who was known for his kindness and good deeds. But my father was dead and I was living with my uncle. So I learned that to survive, I must work. For food, for clothing, I had to earn money. I took any sort of job from anyone who had a job to offer. It was hard. Life in Beersheba was hard. At that time it was a development town. All the European immigrants went to the cities to live. All the Oriental immigrants were sent to the desert. Out of sight, out of mind.

If I hadn't been exceptionally intelligent, my schooling would have ended with my thirteenth year, as in Israel at that time high school was considered higher education and it had to be paid for. But I got a scholarship, much to my uncle's dismay. He wanted to put me out to work so that he could collect my salary. But I attended high school and what little money I did collect went into my secret hiding place for college. My mother had always stressed the value of an education and I would not disappoint even her memory.

The years went by, not happily, not quickly. I became something of an outcast among my fellow Beershebans. I later knew I was just suffering the effects of an unpleasant life. Oh, a couple of times I tried to run away. I should have thought this would please Uncle Elias; but each time I ran, he insisted on finding me and bringing me back. It was during one of these races for freedom that I met my future protector, Amos Bakshi. I was sitting in the police station in Haifa after having been picked up by the police for being vagrant without permission. They were trying to talk my uncle into coming to pick me up. He was telling them it was a day's time wasted and to put me on the bus. They were asking him to send bus fare. He was telling them not to hold their breath. Finally they decided that I should stay overnight in a cell and they would send me south with an army vehicle the next day. That's when Amos stepped in.

"You're going to leave him in jail overnight? For what?"

"For where else to put him," the policeman answered.

"That's ridiculous," Amos said, taking a good look at me. "He can stay at my place."

The policeman had his doubts. "Look, Amos, I feel I know this boy. I've picked him up now three times. He's not the type you want under your roof."

Amos took another look at me and began speaking to me in the Jewish dialect of Iraqi Arabic. "You're Iraqi, aren't you?"

"Yes," I answered.

"So what are you doing in trouble with the police? Iraqis are usually smarter than that."

"I felt the urge to expand my horizons."

"What's wrong with Beersheba?"

"My uncle."

"What's wrong with your uncle?"

"He beats me, he starves me, he belittles me."

"He's your blood. You must go back to him. But tonight you can stay at my place."

"Are you a policeman?" I asked.

"Not exactly," Amos answered. To the policeman he said, "The boy seems fine to me. I'll take him home and bring him back here at seven."

"He's your problem now," the policeman said in a beware-of-the-dog manner.

Amos motioned for me to follow him out of the station, which I did. We walked together in silence up and down the hills of Haifa for half an hour before we reached his apartment. It was a small two-roomer and the kitchen drain didn't work. I had a feeling that Amos's wife wasn't overjoyed to see me. Perhaps it was because I looked like a beggar. My clothes were two sizes too small and tattered from wear. Amos insisted that I remove them all and take a bath. This was an unusual kindness in Israel at the time, as water was scarce and the people took a bath only once or twice a week. Of course I probably reeked so much that there was no other way of dealing with me. (Uncle Elias definitely limited my access to the bathroom.) When I had finished bathing, Amos gave me some old clothes of his to put on. I was not yet taller than he. Meanwhile his wife, Nurit, had washed my clothes and hung them out. I felt like a new person.

For dinner that night Nurit made chicken. I tried to take as little as possible, knowing that with the rationing this would be their only chicken for weeks. But both Amos and Nurit urged me to eat. So I ate while their two children sat on either side of me watching me gorge myself.

That night while Amos's family slept, I couldn't. I was too overwhelmed by gratitude and I wanted to do something to show my appreciation. So I carefully got up from my place on the balcony, tiptoed past Amos and his wife, sleeping in the living room, and made my way to the kitchen. There I closed the door and proceeded to fix the kitchen sink as quietly as I could.

10

I was in the middle of removing the grease from one of the pipes when the door swung open, revealing Amos and an agitated Nurit.

"What the hell are you doing?"

"Unclogging your sink."

"At this hour?"

"I had no other time. I wanted to show my appreciation."

"You scared my wife."

"I'm sorry," I said quietly. "But I'm almost through."

So Nurit put on a pot of coffee and they watched me fix the sink. I learned later that Nurit had been afraid I was stealing their household money, which she foolishly kept in an old cracker tin on the kitchen shelf.

The next morning Amos returned me to the police, who returned me to my uncle, who returned me to hell. But I didn't lose touch with Amos. I wrote to him and he wrote to me. Occasionally I would spend a holiday with them and repair what was needed in their home. During this time Amos moved from Haifa to a small villa outside Tel Aviv and seemed quite prosperous.

Meanwhile I had entered my last year in high school and was intent on entering the university. To do this I had to pass a series of tests given by the army to determine if my usefulness to them would be increased by my further education or not. My skills were obvious. My Arabic was excellent. I had the ability to pick up dialects quickly and to blend into the Arab scene. The army earmarked me for Intelligence. I earmarked myself for economics. Neither of us told the other, so I was allowed my exemption and was accepted on scholarship by the Hebrew University in Jerusalem. With the scholarship and the money I had saved over the years, I would barely be able to make it economically. But that was the condition of nearly everyone in Israel at that time.

The crisis came when my uncle discovered my cash reserves. It was one of those rainy days in Beersheba and I had been out helping someone keep the water out of her flat. I walked in on my uncle as he was counting out my money on his bed.

"Put it back," I screamed at him.

"Nonsense," he said calmly.

"That money is mine!"

"You have nothing except what I give you," he snarled.

I leaned down to scoop up my money from him. It never took much to set Uncle Elias off. He picked up the cane that he kept around for National Health Insurance purposes and struck me a blow right across the kidneys. I fell, in pain. He raised the cane and swung again. He swung and swung and swung in his fury until even his wife was afraid for me. She tried to pull him away, but couldn't. She called the neighbor and together they succeeded in pulling him off. I noticed the cessation more than I had noticed the blows. I must not have moved because I remember the neighbor asking, "Is he . . . ?"

With that I pulled myself into a crouch and managed to propel myself from the room. The rain felt good on my back. It eased the pain. I stumbled my way through the dark streets of Beersheba out into the ever present desert. My life had come to an end. All my dreams of escape lay on my uncle's bed. My will to go on failed me. The desert had been the mother of my teen-age years. I felt the sand come up to comfort me as I lay down on what was to be my grave. I turned over to look up at the sky, the rain pelting me, the stars guiding me to my end. I felt at peace. Drifting off into the end of my existence, I was disturbed only once—by a pair of eyes and a hand that softly shook me. I awoke and knew it was a Bedouin. So let him kill me, I thought. It would have been more fitting to die with my family in Basra, but one Arab hand is much like the other. I fell unconscious again and awoke in a hospital.

When I was able to ask where I was, I found myself in Hadassah Hospital in Jerusalem. It seems I looked so far gone that the soldiers alerted by the Bedouin took me to Jerusalem for the best medical treatment. This far from pleased me, as I was still intent on dying. Annoyed and in pain, I made no effort to communicate with the medical profession attending me. My absence of communication led to their assumption that I was an Arab. My treatment was better for it. We Jews always have the compulsion to prove how humane we are. When they brought in the news photographer to take a propaganda picture— "Arabs Receive Excellent Care at Hadassah"—I screamed something vile at them in Hebrew and they withdrew abruptly. My treatment got worse.

The police came and wanted to know who had done this to me, who my relatives were, all the usual questions. They wouldn't leave me alone. Finally, worn out, I told them they could contact my brother, Amos Bakshi.

When Amos came, he looked at my back and cried. "Your uncle?" he asked.

"Yes," I replied.

He took off. A few days later he came back. "Something smells around here," he pronounced.

"Perhaps it's my dressings," I suggested.

"No. Something smells with this relationship between you and your uncle."

"I have been telling you that for a long time."

"I brought him before the police and he confessed that he beat you, but he still wants you back."

"I won't go."

"Don't worry. I won't let them take you," he assured me. "But the question is why. Why does he want you back?"

"Someone to beat?"

"No. Your uncle looks like the type who does things for only one purpose. Money."

"Well, he never got any from me, except what he stole."

"You have no money?"

"Just what I make."

"You brought none from Iraq?"

"I had to leave in a hurry. My family was dead. I took nothing with me except for my mother's star."

"Was your family wealthy in Iraq?"

"Weren't we all wealthy in Iraq?"

"But your family in particular?"

"I was a child. I didn't know the difference between rich and poor. I had what I needed."

"And what happened to all that you had?"

"The Arabs took it."

"Perhaps. What was your father's name?"

"Solomon Haham."

"I'm going to look into this because something really smells. You concentrate on getting better. I promise you you won't go back to your uncle's."

Amos left. In the week until I was to see him again I made a rapid recovery, cheered on by the thought of never having to see my uncle, and by the plentiful food the hospital provided. I was up and walking when Amos reappeared.

"I've found the answer," he said to me. "But sit down. You are going to be astonished."

I sat down. He looked at me. I looked at him—and waited.

"You are rich."

"But definitely," I scoffed at him. "That's why I'm near starvation and wearing rags."

"Your uncle is the cause of that. Now listen. When you came to Israel and got in touch with your uncle, he, knowing that your father was a rich man, contacted your father's branch office in London. As Elias suspected, Solomon, your father, had had the foresight to move most of his capital out of Iraq and invest it with a London firm. This firm, receiving confirmation of your father's death and your survival, immediately set up a trust fund whereby Uncle Elias would receive the interest to provide for your physical needs and your education. Every month for the last six years he has received a check in the mail from London intended for you, which he naturally deposited in his own account. I have the bank records to prove it. That's why he needed you with him. If you were put under someone else's care, the checks would have stopped coming."

Stunned, I sat there until my anger began to boil within me. The hunger pains, the constant working to get enough decent clothes to wear, the laughter of the other children as I came to school clothed like a crazy man, the physical pains of my uncle's beatings, the mental anguish of being so totally rejected—they all exploded in the pit of my stomach and rose upward.

"I will murder him," I seethed.

"Don't be silly," Amos said rationally. "It's all over now. In two months you'll be eighteen and the trust fund will be yours. If you want to get even with your uncle, throw him in jail."

When it came down to making a decision, I did not have my uncle thrown in jail. I merely insisted that he pay me every cent he had left in the bank. It wasn't much. Uncle Elias had made many investments, most of which failed. Afterward people who did not know criticized me, a rich man, for not helping my uncle, who rapidly returned to his basic hand-to-mouth existence. But I will be the first to admit that I am a vindictive man, and I will never forgive him. Never.

Amos arranged that I stay in a kibbutz for the last two months before my birthday. They were decent to me and I did my share of the work. That summer I turned eighteen, inherited a fortune and joined the army for basic training before I left for the university. But it was not the turning point in my life. No, that came two years later, when I met and married Lison.

Lison was blond and beautiful. Her parents, wealthy French Jews, objected to the match. My skin was too dark. Amos and Nurit objected to the match. Lison was a mental case and was using me to get even with her parents. But I was in my second childhood, not really having had much of a first one, and I saw things as pure or impure. The relationship between Lison and me was pure. We were a perfect match. How wrong I was. I have always thought that perhaps if I had told Lison I was rich things would have gone a little differently. But I was going through a romantic period. I used to think, wouldn't it be a surprise when we both got through the university and I told her I'm rich, that she had really married a prince. I never had the chance.

I had graduated, but Lison was still attending Hebrew University while I was in officers' training for the tank corps. I had managed to elude army intelligence and tanks had become my life. I was really in love with them. I still am. Lison and I had been married two years and I remained desperately in love with her. I made a bore of myself showing off her picture, bragging about what a perfect wife she was.

I was given an unexpected one-day pass so I could surprise her on her birthday. What a surprise. I opened the door on our little one-room apartment in Jerusalem and there she was, sitting on top of Moshe, screwing away. My dreams crumbled along with Moshe's erection. That was the moment when I discovered the truth of my life—it would be destitute of all happiness.

I divorced Lison. Her parents were happy. She married Moshe immediately. I suppose they have a good life together. They have three children. There was no monetary divorce settlement. Later, when her parents found out I was rich, they came around trying to get some money for the divorce. But by that time I was not just rich, I was powerful. I threatened to put her father out of business and onto the streets. They left me alone.

From the breakup of my marriage things tumbled downward. I was kicked out of the tank corps for outmaneuvering a general in war games and rubbing his nose in it. They called it insubordination. I called it brilliance. Army intelligence saw its opportunity and pounced on it. It was then I discovered that my friend Amos Bakshi was in Shin Bet. He had joined the intelligence organization after leaving the Palmach. It seems he had gotten Nurit pregnant and needed some money fast to set up an apartment for her. So he worked inside Jordan for a year

16

while she had their baby. After that he became a control and operated a counterintelligence unit inside Israel to deal with the terrorists. He told me this when he was trying to convince me to go for the academic side of intelligence. But I was on one of my suicide kicks and decided to follow the injunction of Trumpledor. It would be good to die for my country. And I almost did. Many times over.

Following training I was assigned to Captain Dan Tov. He was a vicious bastard with a terrible temper. We got along perfectly. He is one of the few Ashkenazim whom I call my friend. Of course there were rough moments to begin with. When I was first introduced to him, he screamed at me for being a minute late. I had had enough screaming in training so I screamed back, walked out of his office, slammed his door, breaking the glass. At that moment I heard his phone ring. It was Amos telling him to take care of me.

After that we established a good working relationship. Dan had insightful plans, which I refined with my Oriental feel for the situation. My missions took me throughout the Middle East. I always had a weakness for Cairo. On one of my missions I even managed to visit Basra. As had been suggested at the time, the chief of police had taken over my father's house. I roused his family in the middle of the night, sent them outside, then dynamited the house. Those pigs would never again dirty my father's place.

My luck ran out in Algeria. I was caught with my transmitter as I passed on to Israel the contents of a secret meeting between Algeria and top Soviet military officials. Luckily they never found out to whom I was transmitting. I passed myself off as a member of a rival Algerian political faction. At first I was tortured for any political information I might have. After a while I was left alone, to rot, I might add, in a very dirty prison. A year went by before I suddenly found myself released. The rival faction of which I had claimed to be a member had taken over the reigns of government. After my release I made my way from Algeria to France and from France to Israel. When I had received my back pay, a promotion and some dental work, I quit the army.

Throwing myself wholeheartedly into the business world, I expanded my holdings to include companies in most of the European countries and in the Americas. I even established a subsidiary in Iran. But managing my monetary empire soon became automatic and my life lacked excitement. It was then that I decided to use my companies to further Israeli intelligence aims. In each company I placed men whose primary purpose was to conduct a broad range of intelligence-gathering operations which would supplement official Israeli agencies.

As my power and influence spread, I became well known throughout Israel. It was my influence that enabled me to have myself appointed to the tank corps during the Six Day War and it was there that I lost a piece of my gut leading a charge of tanks against the Syrian position on the heights of the Golan. So many good friends were lost there that I could not accept a medal for bravery when it was offered to me. I was guilty and ashamed to be alive when many more valiant men had fallen.

During the Yom Kippur War I rejoined army intelligence, which had been strangled with old men refusing to reevaluate their positions in the face of overwhelming evidence to the contrary. So they were taken by surprise. They worked in their offices to rectify their mistakes while thousands of our young men died. After the war I returned to my companies and my little strategy maps.

Personally I have been far from whole. After losing Lison I could never again become deeply involved with a woman. Not that I didn't want to, but I always drew back at the last minute, afraid again of betrayal, of opening myself once more to be mortally wounded by my own humanity. So I have passed from one woman to another and my reputation as a Don Juan has unfairly grown. Since I am thought of as a perfect lover, I find myself surrounded by women putting me to the test. And my friends regard me with envy. Little do they know how much I envy them in their quiet marriages, sitting down to a sabbath meal with their sons and daughters.

Further on the personal side, I have never forgotten what poverty did to me. Now that I am rich, I make it a point to help my people, the Orientals, survive under Israel's harsh economic conditions. Some people criticize me for not helping the Europeans. But they own the government; they don't need my help. So each week I set aside one day when I see as many as possible of those in need. This is well known in our community and this is the start of the story that I have to tell you.

Chapter 2

IT WAS WEDNESDAY. I always feel that having my public audiences in the middle of the week is the most effective method. It gives me a break from the dismal details of business; also gives me the chance to let off some steam at the official bureaucratic botching up of the lives of my unfortunates. But it was the middle of this particular Wednesday afternoon and even I was beginning to get tired. As usual on these days, I had lunch at my desk to enable me to see as many people as possible.

"Next," I shouted through the intercom, vaguely aware that my shirt had wilted under the exertion of my own good deeds.

The door opened. I focused on my next act of charity. It was not what I had expected. A woman stepped into the room, obviously American of European stock. As I have explained, I don't take Europeans. They have all the protection they need from their own kind. So what was this woman doing here? She must have had a good story to tell or she would never have gotten past my office managers, who are less charitable than I.

I indicated the chair across from my desk. She sat down. A bit chunky, nice breasts, adorable thighs.

"May I see your number?" I said, holding out my hand.

She handed me a slip of paper, on which was written the number 51. I took out my magnifying glass to examine it.

"What are you doing that for?" she asked in English, a language with which I am totally conversant.

I was not used to having my cases open the conversation. Usually they waited until I signaled I was ready. I looked up at her to shame her into silence. She stared back openly at me, not at all submissive, so unlike our own women, who know their place in front of a man.

I decided to be civil. I answered her question. "I am making sure that this is the correct number 51 by examining the paper and the handwriting."

She looked at me as if she thought I was an imbecile. I had to put her straight at once.

"You see, so many times people will forge an early number in order to get in to see me before others."

She twisted her lips and regarded me with what I can only assume was dismay. I decided to overlook her total ignorance of my meticulous methods and get to the heart of the matter.

"How exactly can I assist you?"

"My husband is missing."

"May I see your passport, please?"

"I tell you my husband is missing and you want to see my passport?"

Her voice became grating. Assuming this was from stress, I held out my hand for her passport. She looked for a moment as if she was going to get up and leave, but decided against it, reached into her handbag and delivered her passport.

American, of course. I flipped it open and discovered she was Susan Sasson, age thirty-four, height five feet two inches, weight one hundred fifteen pounds. I think she fudged a little on the weight.

"Your husband is . . . ?"

"Iraqi."

"So you came here."

"Exactly."

"You live here in Israel?"

"No, in America. Ann Arbor, Michigan."

"Ah. Wouldn't it have made more sense to look for your husband in the States?" I suggested as gently as possible.

"He's not there," she said defensively.

"And he is here, then?"

"I don't know. I don't know where he is."

"Perhaps you should tell me a little more about this, um, situation of yours." I glanced at my watch. Another nut case.

"Well, you see," she began falteringly, then stopped. "It's a long story."

"I am here to listen."

"Well, then," she began. "My husband was born in Iraq, in Baghdad, and came to Israel with his family in 1950. He was educated here, went to the Technion, to become an engineer. Then he went into the air force, something to do about programming the computers to locate spare parts for the fighter planes. I don't really know. After serving in Zahal, he left Israel for the Massachusetts Institute of Technology, where he received his Ph.D. I was working in Boston at that time, as a high school teacher. We met at Hillel. He was different. So was I. We were married four months later. Then we moved to Ann Arbor, where he had taken a job as a professor in aerospace engineering at the University of Michigan.

"The first summer we were free, we came to Israel to meet his family. He is the fourth child in a family of six. I liked his family, though I couldn't speak very well with them as I had not yet learned Hebrew. Still, they spoke mostly in Arabic anyway, so it wouldn't have made that much of a difference.

"The years passed, we had two children, he advanced in his job. We visited Israel as often as possible with the prices being what they are. We even spent a year here on our sabbatical.

"It's true I had doubts about my husband. Sometimes I would

wake up at night to hear him talking in his sleep. Occasionally I could recognize some words in Hebrew, also some in Arabic. He uses his languages interchangeably. But several times when I heard him, he spoke neither Arabic nor Hebrew, but a language with which I was totally unfamiliar, had never heard before anywhere. I asked him about this, but he just laughed and said he never heard himself say anything in his sleep. Which was true enough, I suppose. I never pressed him about it. He keeps so much of his life a secret. He's not an open person, not like an American anyway.

"To get to the present situation, well, I guess it started when he sent a New Year's card and it came back. He had sent it to a friend of his in Argentina. They had gone together to the Technion. After graduation his friend had returned to Argentina to take over his father's electronics firm. We couldn't read the Spanish stamped on the letter, so Jacob, my husband, took it to the office, where we had a friend who could read Spanish. He said that it had been stamped 'Address unknown.' Jacob was upset, worried. You know what's happening in Argentina. I suppose we both were afraid that his friend had been killed. Jacob became very disturbed. Sometimes he hardly seemed to notice me. I was surprised because I didn't think he was that close to this friend of his. They only exchanged New Year's cards.

"Then three weeks ago, Jacob got a postcard from Rumania. There was nothing on it. Except our address. And 'Par avion' was written three places on the card, including under the stamps. But there was no message. Jacob claimed to be as puzzled as I was. But two weeks after he received the postcard, he vanished."

There was a silent pause as I realized that she had come to the end of her story.

"You contacted the police?" I asked.

"Yes. They didn't take it seriously. Just said that a lot of men pick up and leave."

"That is true, you know."

"But Jacob isn't like that. He has his job, his home, and even if he were tired of me—I'm not claiming our marriage is perfect —he would never leave the children. You don't know him. He worships the children. He just wouldn't suddenly vanish."

"There is an element missing in your story," I pointed out. "Why would you expect to find him here?"

"Well," she said, trying to speak calmly, "I thought he was spying for Israel, and having collected the information he needed, he had returned here."

"That is a very weird assumption to make about your husband. What possible information could he be picking up at the University of Michigan?"

"Oh, it wasn't there. My husband consults for the United States Army, working in the missile program. Something to do with increasing the effectiveness of the missile delivery system. I don't know exactly, never having paid much attention. I was just glad to have the money coming in. But I know it was something that would prove useful to Israel, because you do use things like Hawk missiles, don't you?"

I decided she did not need enlightening on that subject. "So you came here. And how did you happen to come to me?"

"I contacted Jacob's family. He feels very close to them and I was sure he would get in touch with them if he was in Israel. But they haven't heard from him. I guess I became hysterical when I saw they could give me no help. One of his nephews told me that if anyone could find Jacob, you could. So he came with me early this morning to get in line for a number. And I've been waiting here ever since, waiting to see you."

"Do you have the postcard?"

"What?"

"The one from Rumania."

"Oh, yes," she said, fumbling again in her purse. "Here it is. You can see, it's just as I told you."

"Yes," I said, examining it superficially. "Now I am going to

24

ask you to leave me your telephone number and where you will be staying. There are certain contacts that I can make to clear up the matter of whether or not your husband was working for Israeli intelligence. Until then I have absolutely nothing worthwhile to say to you."

"I understand. I'll be staying with my sister-in-law in Givatayim. Let me write you her address. Do you want me to write it in Hebrew?"

"Either way. Do you know much Hebrew?"

"Enough to be social; not enough to be intellectual."

"Are your children with you?"

"No, they're with my mother in Boston."

"Good. So, Mrs. Sasson," I said, rising, "I will be in touch with you as soon as possible."

"Thank you very much," she said, shaking my hand gently before leaving my office.

Chapter 3

MY DAY LASTED until nine in the evening. By then I was physically tired and emotionally drained. Giving little thought to the problems of Susan Sasson, I dismissed my staff, locked the door of my office, and retreated through Tel Aviv to the cushioned womb of my apartment. There I hid myself behind a cup of tea and my jet-flown copy of the day's *Wall Street Journal* and slid off into sleep. The next day I awoke, my mind as usual invigorated by the night's rest. Reaching for the phone, I dialed the number of Dan Tov.

"Hello?"

"It's David. Did I wake you?"

"Why would you wake me? After all, doesn't everyone get up at five in the morning?"

"Remember the early bird and the worm."

"Am I having them for breakfast?"

"I have a problem for you," I said, pausing for a few moments while his thoughts became professional. Dan Tov had left army intelligence when he discovered that he was not going to become its chief. If he had, I felt sure the Yom Kippur War never would have turned out the way it did. But even after resigning, he couldn't give it up. Espionage was in his blood, as so often happens to those who enter into it young in life. He switched to Mossad and was now one of their senior intelligence officers.

"So." He waited.

"Yesterday an American came to visit me, a Susan Sasson. Her husband is missing and she thinks he might be, to quote her, an Israeli spy."

"Ha. Another one of your nut cases."

"That's what I thought at first. But then she went into some interesting details."

"Like?"

"Like her husband is Israeli, immigrated from Iraq. Now he is an American citizen. When he was in the army here, he worked on our air force computer system. In the States he is a consultant to their army missile command. Seems he disappeared after receiving a postcard from Rumania. No message. Just a postcard. I have it, by the way."

"Hmm. And?"

"And look into it. Is he one of ours? What do we have on him? You know."

"What does the wife want?"

"She wants to know where her husband is."

"Are you sure?"

"I'm calling Amos after you. He'll verify it for me."

"Okay, David. Now that I have this early start, I'll probably be able to take care of it today for you."

"See you."

"Shalom."

After Dan hung up, I dialed Amos's number. Nurit answered.

"Nurit . . . David. Is Amos there?"

"He's been gone all night."

"Oh. At work?"

"So he tells me."

"We'll soon find out. I'll call him there."

"Bye."

"See you."

I dialed the number for Shin Bet. A woman's voice came on the line.

"Number, please?"

"Three seven nine."

"Three seven nine is with two one two."

"Ring two one two, then, please."

"I am not allowed to channel calls through other offices."

"This is seven one two and this is an emergency."

"Just a minute, seven one two."

I heard her plugging through to two one two.

"Two one two," she said, "seven one two is on the line for three seven nine. Emergency."

Two one two handed the phone to Amos.

"Hello."

"Amos, it's me, David."

"David, what the hell are you doing on this line?"

"Would you like my answer numerically or in words?"

"Come on. We're busy. Strategy."

"Something important coming up?"

"David, stop fishing for information."

"Do you know Nurit doesn't believe you're at work?"

"Why don't you go run over there and comfort her?"

"Testy this morning, aren't we?"

"Look, David, I've been up all night; one of our operations is falling apart. I have no time to be pleasant."

"All right, then. I have something for you to check out."

"Okay, give it."

"Jacob Sasson, Givatayim. All of it."

"I'll give it to Baboza. He should be able to run it down in a day. Dinner tonight, my place?"

"Fine."

He hung up.

The day passed in its usual pattern of swerve and financial

counterswerve. Lunch was held with an overseas ice cream firm looking for a co-sponsor to finance a chain of ice cream parlors in Israel. The ice cream was extremely refreshing. I gave the deal a second thought.

I worked late in my office, hoping to catch the call from Dan Tov which never came. Not wanting to push it, I decided to wait till next morning to phone him again. At six-thirty I headed for Amos's.

Nurit opened the door, shushing me as I entered. Amos slept on for another hour while the constant smell of smoldering food came to my nostrils. I accidentally dropped a book smack on their tile floor.

"Shut up in there," a voice came through the bedroom door.

Taking that as a signal that Amos was awake, I entered the bedroom, only to find his eyes looking very glazed over.

"Is it time for dinner yet?" I innocently asked him.

"Go away, David."

"I'm sure you've had a hard day."

"Yes, I have."

I raised my voice. "Nurit, Amos doesn't want any dinner."

"What do you mean, he doesn't want any dinner!" a voice screamed from the general area of the kitchen.

Amos gave me a very nasty look and leaped out of bed.

Nurit's voice came closer. "He calls me this morning telling me to fix something nice. I work all day cleaning the meat and dressing it, besides picking up the house, and now he doesn't want any dinner! Where is he!" The voice became fortissimo.

"Nurit, my darling," Amos said, stumbling over himself to be pacifying, "you know David's sense of humor."

"I don't find it funny," she said.

"Neither do I," Amos agreed.

I got my dinner, an hour late but still pleasantly tasteful.

"So what did Baboza find out about Sasson?" I asked, broaching the subject over a chicken wing.

"Would you wait until I finish my meal?"

29

"I'm sorry, Amos. I had assumed that after you had eaten, you would prefer to go straight back to bed instead of staying up a couple of hours discussing my problems."

Amos rose and got a file from his briefcase.

"Must you read at the dinner table?" Nurit cut in.

"How are the children, Nurit?" I said, distracting her attention from Amos's vicious gaze.

"Both have good steady jobs with sensible hours," she said pointedly.

I turned back to Amos, who had found my report. He handed it to me and I read at the table while Amos and Nurit looked at each other.

Baboza had found nothing extraordinary. According to his report, Jacob Sasson was exactly what Susan Sasson had said he was—an immigrant from Iraq who had left Israel for his graduate studies and never returned. A common enough story. In 1970 he became an American citizen. In 1972 he came to Israel on a sabbatical.

"Nothing much."

"Nothing at all, if you ask me," Amos said. "The wife has a vivid imagination, that's all."

"Perhaps."

"What did Dan say?"

"I haven't heard from him. So you don't have any idea if he reentered the country?"

"Baboza checked passport control. No Jacob Sasson entered in the past two weeks."

"Well, that does it then."

The phone rang. Amos answered it, expecting once more the call to duty. He smiled and looked relieved. Handing me the receiver, he said, "It's Dan. He said he knew you'd be over here mooching a meal."

Taking the phone, I uttered a noncommittal "Yes?"

"David, you hit the jackpot on this one."

"Sasson?"

"Yes."

"He's one of ours."

"No. But he is working for the United States Army in their research and development program."

"Well, I told you he was working for them. The wife wants to know why he disappeared."

"That we don't know. Yet. We're checking it out in the States right now. But we sure would like to find him and they would too—if he is missing."

"Why?"

"Because his latest research project could prove very useful to us."

"Oh. What is it?"

"A ray gun."

"Dan's gone off his rocker again," I said to Amos. Both of us were used to dealing with Dan's debilitating fantasies. "A ray gun," I sneered. "You mean ray gun as in science fiction?"

"Did you laugh when they landed on the moon? Can't talk any more over the phone. Come see me tomorrow morning and I'll give you the dope."

I hung up, not knowing exactly who the dope was going to be.

Chapter 4

I HAD TO GO THROUGH the usual twenty security checks before I reached Dan's office the next morning, but I had a feeling it was going to be worth it.

"So," I said to him as I closed his soundproof door behind me.

Not stopping for the amenities, Dan said, "You see this?" He held up his Wild West revolver, which he had bought several years ago in Texas on one of his infrequent assignments in America.

"Of course I see it. Would you like me to buy you a lasso to go with it?" Dan was very hung up on his macho image.

"Please, I'm being serious now, David," he said, slightly offended. "This is roughly the size of the ray gun that Jacob Sasson was working on. And by the way, my report from America has come in. He is missing. But he took nothing with him. Which means that he has all the information he needs right up here." Dan tapped his head.

"If he took nothing with him, it might also mean he's dead."

"Nope. Don't believe it. Several years ago the United States

Army had developed a laser cannon. Remember the report on it?"

"Yes, of course. It shot a laser beam to bring down a plane, stop a tank, that sort of thing. But most of that work is still in the experimental stages. I mean, it's not being mass-produced."

"Exactly. Well, Jacob Sasson was trying to fit the same principles for the laser cannon into a laser gun."

"Look, Dan, my scientific knowledge is less than impressive, but even I know that it is impossible to get the power source you need for a laser beam to fit into the size of a cap pistol. Those laser cannons you spoke about needed a power source as large as a tank to enable them to work. Even the newer models couldn't be described as lightweight. And they were just developed. Now, if you want to look a couple of decades into the future, you might have something."

"What if I were to tell you that instead of using electricity to power the laser, Sasson was working on an atomic-powered laser."

"I can't believe it."

"Why not?"

"First of all, atomic power is one thing if you have it in a bomb. It's another thing to put it in a little pistol that you carry around with you. Why, they haven't even been able to make a safe nuclear power plant. Second, Jacob Sasson is an aerospace engineer, not a nuclear physicist. Working with atomic power is beyond his scope."

"I'll admit there are several improbabilities involved. But," he said, holding up his hand as he saw I was about to interrupt, "what if he has managed to come across a solution?"

"It's doubtful."

"Not impossible, though."

"Highly, highly improbable. And even conceding that he came across something important, then why did he disappear?"

"Maybe he was dissatisfied with the money and the recognition he was getting from the army."

"Do you honestly think that if he were on to something like a laser gun he wouldn't be given anything he wanted or asked for?"

"Perhaps he had other commitments."

"Dan, you are letting your imagination run away with you. Have you asked, is the United States Army looking for him?"

"Not yet."

"And if he had developed such a weapon, don't you think they would be after him right now?"

"It does present a problem. But only logically speaking. The man was working on a laser gun; the man is missing. I say this is a coincidence we can't ignore."

"And I say that's all it is—a coincidence. Now what should I tell his wife?"

"Don't tell her anything," Dan said.

"Well, I have to tell her something. I promised to call."

"Okay. You call her, tell her you checked with your sources and haven't been able to find out anything. You haven't a clue as to what could have happened to her husband."

"And?"

"And meanwhile," Dan schemed, "I shall put one of my best men on her, and when I say on her, I mean on her." He smiled. "I'm going to get everything out of her that we can."

"This is ridiculous," I said to him.

"Don't question me, David. I'm having one of my hunches."

"Remember that hunch you had when there was a slight earth tremor on the southern border of France? You said France was trying to move the Pyrenees southward to gain more territory."

"That was when I was drunk. I'm sober now. It's nine in the morning."

"Well, it seems to me it's the same sort of idiocy."

"Will you call her?" he asked.

"Yes, I'll call her now. Give me the phone."

I dialed the phone number of Susan Sasson's sister-in-law.

"Hello?"

"Hello. Is it possible to speak to Susan Sasson, please."

"A moment."

"Hello." A rather breathless voice came on the line.

"Hello, Susan?" I asked.

"Yes?"

"This is David Haham. Perhaps you remember me."

"Yes, yes, of course," she said expectantly.

"I've looked into this matter of your husband as far as is possible. I can tell you definitely that he is not an Israeli spy and definitely that he has not come into Israel during the past two weeks. I'm sorry, I just can't give you any idea of where he might be."

"Oh," she said, obviously disappointed and close to tears. "Well, thank you very much for trying to help," she said, breaking down completely. Between sobs she added, "I really appreciate your kindness."

"Look, Susan," I said, "have you checked at home again?"

"I've checked every day, twice a day."

"Nothing?"

"Nothing."

I looked over and saw Dan signaling me to end the conversation. It was hard for me to leave a weeping woman to the tender mercies of his department.

"I'm—I'm really sorry that I wasn't able to help you," I said.

"I know. I don't know what I'll do now," she said, hoping I would have some answer.

"Well, hang in there," I said, giving her meaningless advice. "I'm sure he'll show up on his own sometime soon."

"Yes, perhaps you're right."

"Goodbye, Susan, and good luck."

"Goodbye."

Putting down the phone, I gave Dan a disgusted look, which he failed to notice. He was busy planning his assault on the person of Susan Sasson.

To: Dan Tov
From: Aaron Feldman
Subject: Susan Sasson

Next time give me more warning so I can take my vitamin E shots.

Met subject outside sister-in-law's apartment house. Luckily she was alone. Picked her up. She gave me phony name and ID, Blanche Duboisenbery, divorced from Randy Duboisenbery, Jr., Minneapolis, Missouri, Hadassah member, one great desire in life to see Israel, blah, blah, blah.

Today I took her on the grand tour of Tel Aviv and to dinner at the Casbah. Same spiel from me, same shit from her. Tried to get her in a compromising position this evening. Got a big fat nyet for my efforts. Could I be losing my touch? Maybe she ate too much for dinner.

Try again tomorrow. Expense chit attached. You will note the amount. It's inflation, not greed.

Chapter 5

THREE DAYS LATER I got a phone call from Susan Sasson.

"Hello, Mr. Haham, this is Susan Sasson. Remember? Missing husband?"

"Of course, Susan. What is it?"

"I'm at the police station. I've got one of them."

"One of whom?"

"I can't talk on the phone because there are people listening. But I think it's one of the men involved with my husband's disappearance. Would you come down, please, and help me?"

"Where are you?"

"Oh, it's the police station near King George and Jabotinski."

"I'll be down within the half hour."

Hanging up, I pressed another button, connecting me with my secretary.

"Yes?"

"Call Ron. Tell him to bring the car around immediately."

I don't use a chauffeured car for status. I use it merely because parking is so hard to find in downtown Tel Aviv. Of course if I were really patriotic, I would use the bus; but I didn't have time for the ongoing argument I have with bus drivers who refuse to accept my pass as a disabled veteran. Some friends of mine insist that it is cheap of me to try to get by without paying the bus fare. But first of all, I am entitled to the waiver, and secondly, I always tell them that a penny saved is a penny earned, though that is not original with me.

Ron dropped me off in front of the police station and I galloped in. There was Susan waiting for me on the front bench.

"Thank God you're here," she said. "I don't know how to handle a situation like this."

"Now tell me what happened," I said.

"Well, after you had called, the same evening I was so depressed that I wanted to be alone. So I went out for a walk and was approached by a man who tried to pick me up."

It immediately clicked into my mind what had happened. Dan Tov had sent one of his glamour boys after her, and she had spotted him for a phony.

"And I'm just not the type of woman men pick up."

"Please, Susan, you are too modest."

"Modest, nothing. I've never been picked up in my life. At first I didn't understand what he was trying to do, but when it dawned on me, I thought, well, why not talk to him for a while? You see, I wasn't worried, because he was Israeli and I always trust Israeli men. I suppose that's silly, isn't it?"

"Yes, it is," I agreed.

"Anyway, we walked till we came to a small café, and then we sat and talked for a while."

"You told him about your husband?"

"No. I pretended I was a divorcee on a pilgrimage to Israel. Hadassah member. That sort of garbage."

"Why?"

"Why, what?"

"Why did you lie?"

"My life is really none of his business, is it? So after that he walked me back to my sister-in-law's and said good night. I

38

didn't regret the time I had spent with him. He was very pleasant and distracted me from my problems. But the very next day he showed up again, wanting to know if he could take me on a tour of the art museums. Well, I was surprised, you see, because I was not the greatest company the night before. I thought maybe he was out of work and spent his time as a guide for lonely, middle-aged women. I even hinted at this, and he became sort of insulted. He said he wanted to show me around because he liked me. It was strange, because I usually make a very bad first impression."

"I remember."

"But I had nothing else to do except wait around on the off chance that my husband would show up. So I said why not.

"We spent a pleasant day and had a nice dinner in a restaurant that night. He kept asking a lot of questions about me, but it didn't strike me as unnatural. After all, we knew nothing about each other. But after dinner he tried to, you know, make his move, so to speak."

"Lay you?"

"That's one way of putting it."

"And?"

"Why, what do you mean, and?" she blustered. "And nothing. If you think I came all the way over here looking for my husband just to fool around with another man, you are out of your mind." She paused. "Besides, he's not my type. His skin's too white." She stopped for a minute to consider what she had said. Then she raised her eyes to gaze upon my tanned countenance. "I didn't mean . . ."

"That you like dark men?"

"Right . . . well, actually . . . um. I mean, you see . . ."

"It's quite all right, Susan. I myself prefer blondes, women of about your coloring. Opposites do attract."

"Well, I'm glad you understand what I meant. Anyway, should I go on with what happened?"

"Please."

"After he took me home and left, I began to think that this whole relationship was very peculiar. Here he was a stranger showing me Israel and asking me all these questions. Here I was in Israel looking for my husband and believing him to be involved in espionage activities. It became too much of a coincidence. I saw his attentions for what they were, a ruse, concealing his true mission, which I believe has something to do with my husband. So this morning when he came, as I knew he would, I was determined to get to the bottom of the whole situation. I asked him to take me to the City Hall square because I knew that there had to be some police around. Then when we were in the middle of the square, I started hitting him with my purse, screaming rape and murder and theft. Sure enough, the police came. They have him in custody now."

"Have you thought of what you are going to do if he actually turns out to be just a man interested in your company?" I asked.

"Oh, but I'm sure he's not."

"And if he is?"

"Well, maybe I can just make up some story about like how I was once attacked in New York City and I've had these seizures ever since. How's that?"

"Fascinating," I said. "Let's go see this companion of yours."

Chapter 6

I RECOGNIZED HIM the moment I saw him. It was Pretty Boy Aaron Feldman of the one hundred and one positions. Actually he works out in the gym at the same time I do, keeping his body firm and his arrow quivering under the hand of the masseuse.

"Is this the man?" I asked Susan.

"Yes."

I turned to the police and said, "Officer, have you checked his fingerprints against your file?"

"What do you mean, checked his fingerprints? I just brought him in here."

Aaron bounced up. "Come on, David, cut the crap. Telephone Dan and get me out of here."

"You know as well as I do, Aaron, that in our profession we all have to take risks." I took Susan by the arm and led her out of the cell area.

"You knew that man," she said to me accusingly.

"Yes."

"Well?" She waited.

"Well, what?"

"Don't you think you owe me some sort of explanation?"

"I don't owe you any explanation, Susan. But I am going to put you in touch with the man who does."

We walked out of the police station. Ron, efficient as usual, pulled up smoothly alongside us. Getting into the car, I told Ron to drive toward the Yarkon. Then I picked up my car phone and dialed Dan Tov.

"Hello."

"Dan, this is David."

"Yes?"

"I'm in the car with Susan Sasson. Aaron Feldman is in jail. Do you want to talk about it?"

"Christ!"

"Well?"

"Where?"

"My place or yours?"

"I'll be in your office in fifteen minutes."

Dan must have huffed and puffed to get there, because by the time I had settled Susan into one of my well-padded armchairs, my intercom sounded, informing me that Dan Tov had arrived.

"So," he gasped.

"Susan Sasson, Dan Tov," I made the introductions.

"What happened to Aaron?" Dan asked once he had lowered his bulk into a chair across from Susan.

"Mrs. Sasson caught on to Aaron. Furthermore, she doesn't like his type. She prefers the darker races, don't you, Susan?"

"Usually," she said, "unless it's someone exceptional."

"So now she wants to know what this is all about," I continued. "Are you going to tell her?"

Susan waited; I waited; Dan decided. He turned to Susan and said, "We think we know why your husband disappeared."

"Yes?" she said expectantly.

"We believe he has developed a ray gun."

It took Susan about a two-second reaction time before she burst into hysterical laughter. Dan lifted himself angrily out

42

of his chair and stormed around the room until Susan subsided.

"Are you from Israeli intelligence?" she asked him.

"Yes."

"Well, what kind of Mickey Mouse operation are you running!" she asked angrily. "Ray gun! You asshole. My husband's never even managed to unplug the kitchen sink. He can hardly walk up the stairs without tripping over his own feet. He is a first-class klutz. And you're talking about his making a ray gun. Jesus. You're disgusting."

"Dan was one of my sources in checking on your husband, Susan. He came up with this theory of his about a ray gun. To see if you had any more information to give, he put Aaron on to you."

Susan sighed and held her head. Dan prepared for a counteroffensive. Pulling his chair closer to Susan's, he began.

"Just because your husband's a klutz doesn't mean he can't have a brilliant mind. Now, I know for a fact that he was working on a laser-beamed gun for the United States Army."

"Look, Mr. . . . ."

"Dan."

"Look, Dan, I don't know much about my husband's work for the army, but I do know this: He never worked on any complete project. He only worked on a very, very small section of any project he was assigned to. He is an aerospace engineer. He works on guidance and control, not lasers. I want to find my husband, that's all. When I asked David for help, I didn't think I would become involved in this type of farce."

"All right. So why do you think your husband disappeared?" Dan attacked.

"I don't know why. My theory is that while working on the missile program, he discovered something that he thought would be of value to you and came here to pass it on. Or something. I just don't know."

"Well, that theory is no good," Dan said. "If the United States happens upon something important to do with its missiles, we don't need spies to find it out. They pass it on themselves. The Middle East has become a testing ground for both Soviet and American weapons, or haven't you been reading the papers?"

"Well," I cut in, "I think both of your theories are way off. I know this is hard to face, Susan, but isn't it just possible that he ran off with another woman?"

"You don't know him," she protested. "He's just not the type."

"Every man's the type," Dan cut in. "Even though I'm still going for the ray gun."

"He doesn't even work with any woman. Where would he meet one?"

"For your age, you are very naïve," Dan said.

"I'm no match for you," she sniffed.

"Could we stop this childishness," I demanded. "We still have a missing husband. The only real lead we haven't followed up on is this friend of his—from Argentina, wasn't it?"

"Yes."

"Who disappeared. And then the postcard from Rumania. Hmm. Did you notice if your husband's passport was missing?"

"The police asked me that too. I don't know where he keeps it."

"You don't? Why not?" I asked.

"Well, you see, Jacob keeps track of everything. He has all the important papers in files. I don't really pay much attention to them."

"That's not very wise, is it?"

"Perhaps not. But keeping track of things just isn't what I like to do."

"Well, then I hope we can find your husband. Wait a minute. Did you notice, was there a large sum of money missing?"

"No. I checked that. No money missing."

"Did he have an account on the side?"

"No, he couldn't have had. His monthly check goes straight to the bank. He doesn't make that much."

"And clothes. What kind of clothes were missing?"

"A few suits, some underwear and his topcoat."

"So he could have gone anywhere."

"Yes."

We were all despondent. I fiddled with my pencil, then opened my top drawer, bringing out the postcard from Rumania. I gave it to Dan and said, "Is there anything you notice right off?"

Dan examined it. "It's a picture of a column in Bucharest during a May Day celebration. That's all I can see."

"What do you mean, May Day?" I pounced.

"Well, I'm assuming it's May Day. I mean, there are all these flags, all these people, and the pictures of Lenin. Rumania wouldn't be celebrating the Russian liberation of Czechoslovakia. Conclusion: It's May Day."

"And today," I said, flipping the calendar, "is April 29. Pack your bags, Susan. We're going to Rumania."

"David," Dan said, "be sensible. It's just a postcard. Besides, you will hardly be welcomed in Rumania. They're sure to have you on file and you can bet your bottom kopeck you won't be greeted with open arms."

"But my file is closed, Dan. I haven't been an operative for years."

"Once a spy, always a spy. You're asking for trouble."

"I've always been able to take care of myself. And who knows. Perhaps the visit might prove profitable. Perhaps I'll open a chain of felafel stands throughout the countryside. Businessmen with capital are welcomed anywhere. Well, what do you say, Susan? Is it Rumania?"

"But aren't they communists. I mean, will my country let me go there?"

"My dear, dear simple naïve child of the fifties. There is no more cold war. We fly to Rome immediately and make our connection from there. Agreed?"

"Agreed," she agreed. "Will we find my husband?"

"It is our final clue, Susan. We must follow it up."

★ II ★
Europe

To: Shimshon Shapira
           Israeli Embassy
           Bucharest, Rumania
From: Dan Tov
cc.   Haim Zion, Minister of Defense
Subjects: David Haham
           Susan Sasson

   Subjects on way to Rumania to look for Jacob Sasson, husband of Susan. Keep an eye on them.

Chapter 7

ON MAY DAY Susan and I rose early and left our adjoining rooms in a Rumanian hotel which I had fondly renamed the Comrade Hilton. We made our way down to the square pictured in the postcard and found we were not the first to arrive. The souvenir sellers were already planting their makeshift kiosks along the sidewalks in hopes of catching the earliest vacationers enjoying their workers' holiday.

I myself was in an excellent mood, breathing deeply, enjoying the smell of the hunt with a picture of Jacob Sasson lining my pocket. Susan was a little bit unsure of herself, afraid of not speaking the language, afraid of the iron curtain, of the strangeness of her surroundings. As we reconnoitered the square, she stuck very close by me.

"They look normal," she said to me.

"Who?" I asked.

"The people."

I laughed. "How did you expect them to look?"

"Oh, sort of grim and drab, with pairs of secret police tramping up and down checking papers. But the women, they're all dressed in gay colors with bright scarves. It's really rather pleasant."

"But you're still scared."

"Yes. I feel that if I made the slightest wrong move, I would be thrown into jail and no one would see me again."

"Look."

"Oh," she gasped, grabbing my arm as two policemen crossed our path. They gave her a look of inquiry, then went on their way.

I laughed at her. "You see, they knew you were a tourist and they wouldn't think of stopping you. You're bringing money into the country. So be brave. Everything will be all right."

She smiled, reassured, while I considered our situation. Tactically we were going to have a problem. I could see that right off. The column in the center of the square was fat and pudgy, like a matron resting on her haunches. Thus there was nowhere we could place ourselves to view the entire square at one time. We would have to split up. Circling the square twice, I noticed two obvious meeting places. One was a sidewalk café standing out in front of a three-story hotel, the other a small eatery, a few tables in front of a tobacco shop. I explained the situation to Susan.

"You take the café," I told her. "I'll take the tobacconist's."

"But what'll I do there?" she whined.

"Sit down and order breakfast," I said.

"And then what?"

"Then eat and have a few cups of coffee."

"Alone?"

I went into the tobacconist and bought her a few magazines in French and several in English.

"Read them," I said, thrusting them at her. "And keep a sharp eye out for your husband. I'll be here all the time looking for him too."

"And what if I see him?"

"If he is alone, confront him. If he is with someone, follow

51

him. Chances are that he'll circle partway around the square and I'll spot him too."

"Okay," she said apprehensively. "You mean I'm to sit there all day?"

"And all night if need be. If nothing comes up, I'll meet you back at the hotel."

"All right," she said. She started off hesitantly at first, then grasping her magazines, marched more forcefully around the square to her café.

The hours passed waiting and watching at the tobacconist were far from unpleasant. By midmorning the square had filled with people—families out for a stroll, young couples holding hands and gazing at each other, youths dressed in Levi's and bent on acting tough. Of course I was not in my prime. I'll admit I fidgeted. At the height of my career I could have waited twenty-four hours for someone and not noticed the time passing. It's an art. Soon lost without practice. In those days I worked without a partner, if that's what one could call Susan Sasson. Not that I didn't trust other people. I was just a loner and everyone knew I worked better that way.

The afternoon was beginning to falter toward five o'clock when I first spotted him coming from a side street into the square. Mohammed Sadeq, Palestinian firebrand, cut his teeth on plane hijacking, now graduated to strategy planner for Black September. To find him in Bucharest on May Day was more of a surprise than it would have been to see him in Tel Aviv on Independence Day. Still, the PLO was trying to enlarge its diplomatic contacts and nothing should have surprised me. He looked around the square till his eyes locked onto the tobacconist sign; then he headed my way.

I was not afraid of being recognized. I was too old for him by at least ten years. And I was no longer a threat, being no longer active. My eyes took on the disinterested gaze of a bored drinker wasting a few hours before going home for the evening. I was rewarded by Mohammed's taking a seat at the next table.

52

He ordered a drink in German, took a few sips, then nervously glanced at his watch.

Ten minutes later his waiting was over. An Arab of indiscriminate origin walked by the tobacconist, gave Mohammed a slight nod, then walked away down the second side street. Mohammed hastily paid his bill and followed, not even bothering to finish his beer. Sloppy work. Easily spotted. I casually paid my bill and followed after Mohammed. No doubt the tobacconist was glad to see the last of me. I wondered fleetingly how Susan was doing. If her husband had shown up, I hadn't seen him, and I doubted whether she had either. In a way this was just a final fling at finding Jacob Sasson, following a final clue. I had my doubts that we would ever find him, unless he wanted to be found, or unless by some chance Mohammed led me to him.

I followed Mohammed, who followed his Arab friend. Our trek was not far. Eleven blocks, to be precise. Eleven blocks to the Soviet embassy. Mohammed joined his friend at the gate, and both were escorted inside. I stood in the shadows waiting for them to come out. Perhaps they would come out alone, perhaps with a member of the embassy staff. It was the staff member I was waiting to see. From him I could somehow gauge what our Arab brethren were up to. Unfortunately the two Arab brethren in the embassy were less important at that moment than the one who stood behind me.

Chapter 8

I WAS ALERT ENOUGH to turn facing him before he came up to me, but I was not alert enough to take any fighting stance. So out of practice was I that I was wide open to attack. Luckily attack was not what he had in mind.

"David?"

"Ali?"

We didn't exactly fall on each other and embrace, but we knew each other well. Or at least we knew each other's work well.

Ali Gamel, Egyptian. When I was in service, I knew he spent much of his time programming his men for infiltration into Israeli development towns. If they were young enough and without a family, our army, glorious Zahal, would draft them into service. The infiltrators would then pass sensitive material into the hands of Ali Gamel and Egypt. Sometimes we caught his "students," sometimes not. Even now we don't know how many infiltrators are still inside Israel, enjoying what I like to think of as a more comfortable standard of living than they would have had in Egypt. Perhaps they are even beginning to think like Jews since they, like us, must be constantly looking over their shoulders.

And Ali knew of me, mainly for my work inside Egypt. Matter of fact, when I retired from the army, in an unbecoming fit of sheer invincibility I sent a picture of myself I had had taken in front of the pyramids to Gamal Nasser. I understand he was quite perturbed, though appreciative of my skills.

"Nice finally meeting you," I said to Ali, holding out my hand. I am not one to bear a grudge against a single man for the actions of a whole country.

He took my hand and said, "So you are more amenable now that we beat the shit out of you."

"Enjoy your misplaced self-confidence, dung of the earth; it won't last for much longer."

That out of the way, we turned our attention back to the Soviet embassy. Still no action there.

I turned back to Ali and said, "You're late. Your friends are already inside with Big Brother."

He stood impassive at my side; I could see that he also was watching for the exit from the embassy.

We waited together as the day slowly faded. If it got any darker, we wouldn't be able to tell who was coming out or going in. A dim light went on in the guardhouse near the embassy gates.

Mohammed came through the doorway first, followed by his Arab friend. Last through the door was a tall, hulking blond with crew cut, obviously Russian. He wore a topcoat and smoked a cigarette. All three stopped in the middle of the embassy courtyard and chatted. Then their meeting broke up with waves and smiles. Mohammed and his friend walked past the gate. The Russian got into an official chauffeured limousine and pulled through the gate after them. Ali was standing at my side, taking pictures of the whole gathering with his Minox.

Having no camera with me, I stood by, envious.

When the embassy had returned to its inactivity, I said to Ali, "Meet me at the café in the square at ten tomorrow morning."

He looked up, puzzled. I smashed him into unconsciousness, grabbed his camera and ran—straight to the Israeli embassy. I was not exactly welcomed with open arms. The embassy was staffed with the same lazy bureaucrats that staff the home front. But I found the man I wanted. Shimshon Shapira, commercial liaison and organization man. He did not seem surprised to see me, until I told him my story.

"I knew Mohammed Sadeq was in the country," he said, "but why is anybody's guess."

"Can you develop the film?" I asked.

"Right now."

We went to the lab and stood around making small talk while the film was developed. The frames were strikingly clear. Ali was a good photographer.

"Do you know them?" I asked Shapira.

In answer he picked up the phone, dialed an extension and spoke. "Check this license number for me."

Two minutes later we had the answer.

"It's as I thought," Shapira said. "Kolonikov, Red Army military supplier to the sufferers of oppression in the Third World."

"Great."

"The possibilities of the situation are less than pleasing."

"And the other Arab?" I asked.

"Tewfiq Hassani, Syrian junta member, attached to military planning."

"Something smells."

"Bad."

"Another giant step for détente."

"Step all over us anyway. As is usual. And Ali didn't join them?"

"No," I said. "Waited outside, taking these pictures."

"That's an interesting point to look into."

"I'm meeting him at the café in the square at ten tomorrow."

"Don't show up first."

"I won't."

"We'll have you covered."

"Good."

I left Shapira to ponder his problems and transmit the information to Tel Aviv. Returning to my hotel, I discovered I was not through for the night. I had a hysterical woman on my hands.

She burst through our connecting door the minute she heard me.

"You found him!"

"No," I said, taking off my shoes, the first act of a tired man.

"But where were you? I went to the tobacco shop when the café closed. You were missing."

"Right. I deserted my post."

"It's not funny," Susan said tearfully.

"Look, Susan, I saw someone I knew that at the time seemed more important to me than your husband. So I followed him."

"An Arab?"

"Yes."

"But my husband?"

"Is missing. You didn't see him. I didn't see him. Go home, Susan. Go back to Ann Arbor and wait for him there."

"But you said . . ."

"I said this was our last chance and it just didn't pan out. I'll arrange for your flight tomorrow. All right?"

"All right," she said in a voice so low I barely heard her. Then she walked back into her own room and lay down on the bed. I had half a mind to go comfort her, but decided to save my strength for tomorrow, when I would surely need it dealing with Ali.

To: Ovadia Gelfman, Chief, Section 2–7
               Haim Zion, Minister of Defense
From: Shimshon Shapira
Subject: David Haham

Haham has observed, along with Ali Gamel, Egyptian, a meeting between Kolonikov, Tewfiq Hassani and Mohammed Sadeq that took place on Russian embassy grounds. Photographs on way via courier. David has meeting set up with Ali Gamel for tomorrow morning.

Please advise.

To: Shimshon Shapira
From: Ovadia Gelfman

Let David handle situation. Transmit *immediately* whatever he gets.

To: Shimshon Shapira
From: Haim Zion, Minister of Defense

What happened to Susan Sasson? Her name is not mentioned in your report. Is she still in Rumania? Is she still with David? Find out and report immediately. If she is still with David, suggest he stick with her. Reply on this only to me. Confidential and urgent.

Chapter 9

I GOT SUSAN UP EARLY, fed her breakfast, and arranged for the first flight out of Bucharest to Rome and from Rome to Boston. We packed her things and then I escorted her to the taxi service, placing her in one and sending it on its way to the airport. I mumbled a few apologies about not being able to find her husband. She mumbled a few thanks for the effort. Then I prepared myself for my meeting with Ali, an hour and a half away.

I arrived at the square at ten and took the precautionary measure of circling the square twice to see the setup. Ali had already seated himself at the café and as far as I could see, he had no men placed in any of the obvious shoot-out positions. I came over and joined him.

"So," I said, stretching my body back and ordering an espresso.

"So," Ali said to me. "How were the pictures?"

"Excellent, Ali, really excellent."

"I'm so glad to hear that."

"The Russian in the limo was Kolonikov, Red Army. You

know Mohammed, of course, and the other Arab?"

"Tewfiq Hassani, Syrian," he snapped.

"Ah, then they are all friends of yours. So why did you need the pictures?"

"To pressure the right people." He stopped for a moment, looking at me with distaste, then said, "I have been authorized by my government to let you in on a few important facts of life for both of us. If we both don't move quickly, there is going to be another war."

He stopped to see if I had heard him. I assured him he had my fullest attention.

"War," he continued, "will break out against Israel on three fronts, or so it is planned: the Syrian front, the Egyptian front and"—he paused—"the Lebanese front."

"Lebanese?" I questioned.

"Palestinians," he answered.

"The Palestine Liberation Organization?"

"So we assume."

"They have no combat-hardened fighting units."

"So we assumed."

"They would be slaughtered in a regular military campaign."

"The Russians are trying to convince them otherwise."

"And how are they doing that?"

"By promising to supply them with all the current military equipment."

"And what will they do with their rockets and mortars without an air force to back them up?"

"The Russians will fly for them under the Syrian insignia."

My thoughts were not comforting. "And Syria?" I asked.

"Syria will come into the war because Russia has promised to equip her with SAM-12's to protect her populated areas."

"SAM-12's?"

"Laser-guided missiles."

I thought about that for a moment. "And Egypt?"

"Egypt," he spit out, "according to the Soviet game plan, will be dragged into the war by the Syrians and the Palestinians in the hopes, first, that it can gain back the Sinai, and second, so that it can maintain its preeminence in the Arab world."

"And when is this war to take place?"

"Never. If we can stop it."

"Never?"

"Look, David, you think it is easy for us to make war, that we are bloodthirsty savages. I have read your propaganda and I know that this is what you believe. But we are not a war-loving people. And we have problems at home that must be solved now if Egypt is ever going to make its way into the modern world."

"Very pretty," I said to him. "Aren't you omitting the main reason why you don't want war?"

"And what is that, Jew?"

"You don't have the equipment. We'd slaughter you. This is the Russian way of evening the score for your rapprochement with the West."

"I like my reasoning better."

"I'm sure you do," I said. "But to squabble now is a childishness we can't afford. Do you have any plans to stop this Russian-designed war?"

"Stop the equipment flow, you stop the war."

"And how do you propose to do that?"

"Tell the United States."

"Did Big Daddy ever step in when the Russians were shipping arms to you and the Syrians? So why would they step in now? Diplomatically we can use their leverage. But to stop a war we must do it ourselves."

"How?"

"First, let us consult our governments further, especially since I have no idea how much of this mine knows about. Second, I think it would be advisable to attack the weakest member in this chain of war, the Palestinians. Can you give any help there?"

Ali thought, then said, "The Palestinian factions are holding a meeting next week in Paris. This is to get a consensus on the fighting itself. They are so far afraid to tackle the political settlement afterward."

"Then Paris should be our first line of attack."

"Agreed."

At that point we heard a car screeching up in front of the café. Obviously both of us were afraid that the other had planned a public execution, as we both fell flat underneath the table. Gazing at each other through the table legs, Ali and I realized our mistake. We started to get up. I didn't make it. A handbag came smashing down on my head.

"You knew where he was! You knew where he was and you didn't tell me! You bastard! You dirty, stinking, rotten bastard!"

I looked up and there was Susan Sasson, gone mad. She was swinging both her bag and her suitcase at me and screaming all the time. Ali had disappeared and I was left alone with this crazed animal. I made a run for it around the square, but she followed more quickly than one would expect.

Chapter 10

HOW HUMILIATING. I would be the laughingstock of the whole espionage community. My shame mingled with my fury, and as soon as Susan had followed me far enough into a deserted side street, I turned and charged at her. Startled, she broke her pace and stopped her flailing long enough for me to grab her arms and thrust her up against the side of a building.

"Just what the hell do you think you're doing?" I snarled at her.

"Get your hands off me, you pig, you filthy, filthy liar."

"Do you know what you just did back there?" I asked her. "You just happened to break up an important conversation that might mean Israel's survival."

"Don't overrate yourself, you sagging, pretentious he-man."

I stepped back in astonishment. How dare this twerpy American who was at least twenty pounds overweight call me sagging? I was trim and fit, from working out in a gym every possible day.

Taking advantage of her release, Susan straightened her clothes, then picked up her bag and suitcase. Looking at me fiercely, she said, "Okay. The game is up. Now take me to my husband."

I looked at her in disgust. This girl was a broken record. "For the last time, Mrs. Sasson," I stressed, "I don't know where your husband is. And furthermore, I don't care."

"You would make a good actor, Mr. Haham, but I happen to know that you are lying. You most certainly do know where my husband is because you saw him yesterday."

"Bullshit. Who told you that?"

"William O'Brian."

"William O'Brian," I mimicked. "What is he, a leprechaun, that he should know so much?"

"No, he's CIA."

That shook me. "CIA, Bill O'Brian?"

"That's right. So you can cut the phony pretending, 'cause I don't believe you any more."

"You would believe a Bill O'Brian over David Haham, one of your own?"

"You've got it now."

"Look, I don't know what kind of game you're playing or he's playing, but let me assure you, I do not know where your husband is."

"You're lying."

"Why do you think I would lie to you, Susan?" I said, trying to be reasonable, always a mistake with a woman.

"Because my husband was kidnapped by the Russians to help them build their SAM-12 missile, which is laser-guided, the same sort of missile he was working on in the States. And yesterday you stood outside the Soviet embassy and saw my husband being dragged into a limousine there to be taken to the airport for a flight to Moscow. And now you are working with Shimshon Shapira in the Israeli embassy here, plotting to rekidnap my husband from the Russians and take him to Israel, where you expect him to continue his work for you."

"Bill O'Brian told you all that, didn't he?"

"Yes," she affirmed. "And you're not denying it, are you?"

"How can I? O'Brian has skillfully woven several facts into this fairy-tale fabric, which give credence to his whole story. Of course his whole story is ridiculous."

"He said you would say that."

"First of all, how important is your husband—not to you, to the military-industrial complex at large? Not very, let's admit it. Second, why would the Russians kidnap your husband and leave him lying around Rumania for a week—"

"Plastic surgery to change his appearance so no one could recognize him," she interrupted.

"—when they could simply ship him to Moscow directly. And lastly, how could even you possibly think that we Israelis could go into Mother Russia to rekidnap your husband? Such stupidity is only believable at the height of a UJA pledge dinner."

"You have a way of twisting words, I'll admit that. But O'Brian said to me, 'Stick close to Haham; he'll take you to your husband.' And that's exactly what I intend to do."

"And I suppose during all this time you're sticking close to me, you will be simultaneously reporting on my every action to Bill O'Brian and men of his ilk."

"Yes," she admitted.

We were at a standstill. She wouldn't leave me because even though I had planted doubts in her mind about the veracity of one Bill O'Brian, I was still the last straw she could clutch at in her search for her missing husband.

I decided to take a step that would at least turn her in a more favorable direction.

"Okay," I said.

"Okay, what?" she asked.

"Okay, we'll go to the Israeli embassy and see Shimshon Shapira."

"Really?"

"Yes."

"Then it's true what O'Brian told me?"

"No," I said. "But I want you to find that out for yourself firsthand."

We went together to the Israeli embassy, located Shapira, and together told him the story.

"O'Brian, yes," Shapira said thoughtfully. "He's a regular in the Eastern bloc."

"Can you contact him?" I asked.

"I can contact him, yes. What kind of contact do you want?"

"By phone and now," I said.

"That might prove difficult."

"Look, Shimshon," I said, even in front of Susan, "I haven't given you my report on my meeting with Ali, but when I do, you'll see that we have no time to play games with the O'Brians of this business. I want to straighten Susan out now."

Shapira picked up his phone and dialed. When he got his number, he said, "May I please speak with Mr. Johnston." He paused. "Ollie, this is Shapira. Yes, fine, and you? Good. We seem to be having a little problem here with one of your men and one of ours. I think it would be beneficial to both of us if we straightened it out. Yes. With whom? A William O'Brian. Is there a number where he can be reached? He's there now? Well, our man is here now. Can we put them on? Yes? Good. Just a moment." Shapira handed me the phone while putting the call on the speaker, enabling all of us, especially Susan, to hear the ensuing conversation.

"O'Brian," I snapped.

"Yes," came a cheerful voice. "This isn't David Haham, is it?"

"You know damn well it is. What's the meaning of sticking this girl on me?"

"Clever, wasn't it? Where is she now?"

"In the outer office."

"Good. You'll learn to love her."

"What's the point?"

"The point is, my dear Israeli friend, that we, your American supporters, thought that we could rely on you, our dear Israeli friends, to keep us informed on what the Russkis, your detested enemies, were up to in your area. Now, as it turns out, we had to rely on the Egyptians for certain information about a certain proposed war plan and certain new weapons which we should have gotten long ago from you."

"We are not invincible, you know. I just found out that certain information you are referring to myself and was about to pass it along the chain when your girl pounced on me."

"I'll have to agree with the girl there, Dave—you are a filthy swinish liar. Anyway, at least we now have a close source of information on you."

"Don't you think it's despicably cruel to use the Sasson woman this way?"

"Where there's hope, there's life. So I'm doing her a favor," Bill O'Brian assured us all.

"By the way, what did happen to her husband?" I asked.

"We're checking on that now. The one fact we have is that a few days ago he bought two tickets for a romantic May flight to Paris. So we think he has a bimbo on the side."

"No!" Susan started to scream out. Shimshon rushed to silence her.

"What?" O'Brian asked.

"I said, 'Oh.'"

"Oh. Yes, shocking, isn't it? Well, them's the ways of the world. How you gonna keep them down on the farm and all that."

"Yes. Quite. Don't you think you should call her off? She might get hurt."

"I'll depend on your gallantry to protect her," he said as he hung up.

Susan, Shimshon and I looked at each other as I put down the phone.

"Well?"

"Well?"

"Well?"

"Susan, could you wait outside while Shimshon and I discuss the situation?"

"Yes, of course," she said. "I'm sorry I caused you so much trouble."

"I am too," I assured her.

After she left, Shimshon said, "So?"

"So," I said, "let's sit down and I'll tell you what's with Ali."

We sat down together and I gave him the whole story up until the time of the attack by the outraged wife. That brought a few chuckles, not from me. Now we had to plan our course of action.

"I'll send this information to Tel Aviv," Shimshon assured me. "But until they get it, evaluate it and formulate a plan of action, why don't you fly to Paris and keep up with Ali?"

"Yes, I was thinking that myself. We've established contact and a certain rapport, however weak it might be."

"I'm sure Mossad will send other operatives and have the area well covered. But every little bit helps and Ali seems to be Egypt's main man on this case."

"He's trustworthy for them," I said.

"Yes," Shimshon agreed.

"So I go to Paris."

"With the Sasson woman, don't you think?"

"Why?"

"The CIA will be making contact with her. She can be used."

"She's been used enough."

"What did O'Brian say? Her husband may be in Paris."

"With another woman."

"Perhaps now she'll feel vengeful, not only against her husband but also against the CIA. I might have put it wrong. She can be used, but she can also be useful. Anyway, she has to get to Boston somehow, so fly with her to Paris. See what develops."

"I'm putting her on the first plane home," I told him.

"See what develops," he said, looking at me with a slight smile.

To: Ovadia Gelfman, Chief, Section 2–7
             Haim Zion, Minister of Defense
From: Shimshon Shapira
Subject: David Haham

Following is David's report of his meeting with Ali Gamel. As you can see, things don't look good. I have been able to discover nothing so far. It seems to me that the only event of importance that took place in my territory was the meeting at the Soviet embassy.

David is flying to Paris after Ali. They are going to try to deal with the Palestinians. I suggested to David that you would have men there to supplement him, not that he thinks this is necessary.

To: Haim Zion, Minister of Defense
From: Shimshon Shapira
Subject: Susan Sasson

Subject has been approached by the CIA in an attempt to turn her in their favor. It worked for a while until she heard her CIA control discussing with David his devious conning of her.

Now she is flying with David to Paris. I suggested to David that he keep her close by. He resented the suggestion and plans to send her packing to Boston as soon as they land in Paris.

CIA reports that subject's husband has been seen buying two tickets to Paris. They theorize he is with a woman.

Subject seems in no emotional position to do much damage to our cause.

To: Dan Tov, Chief, Section 6–3
From: Haim Zion, Minister of Defense
Subject: Operation Paris Triangle

Contact Ovadia Gelfman and review Shapira's reports and other relevant information. Then fly to Paris and take charge of this operation.

I am assuming you can handle Haham.

Chapter 11

SUSAN, TOTALLY DEPRESSED, was not about to make a joyful traveling companion to Paris. Still, her silence had its advantages in allowing me to easily maneuver our way through Rumanian officialdom and into the airplane. She sank further into herself. Even with the first-class accommodations I had arranged for us. I watched the remaining passengers board the flight and was glad to spot no one of particular interest.

Once up in the air, I ordered drinks for both of us, hoping that would at least loosen Susan slightly from her depression. I took her hand in what I thought to be a comforting fashion. She withdrew it immediately, turning her body away from me and looking out the window. I hated to see her so down all the time.

"What's the matter?" I asked as gently as possible.

" 'What's the matter?' What a stupid question."

"I'm only trying to make you feel better," I said defensively.

"Well, you can't make me feel better, so leave me alone."

"Why are you upset? Because your husband ran off with another woman?"

"Do you realize how humiliating this all is. If I had known, I

70

never would have tried to find him."

"If you had never tried to find him, we would have never met," I said, trying to interject a romantic note to cheer her up.

"Big loss for both of us," she murmured.

"Anyway, I think your husband was a fool to leave you."

"But you don't know, do you? You don't know a thing about our marriage. Well, let me tell you about it," she said, turning to face me. "Like all marriages, it started off with a wedding. Then the children came, one after the other. What a happy little picture postcard we all made. While I stayed home to take care of the children and give them the solid emotional background they needed to grow up into middle-class prodigies, my husband traipsed off to work each morning, no doubt enjoying himself tremendously. And when I began to turn into an aging hausfrau due to the fact that I gave up my own life for his, he found someone more exciting and less stupid. Together they are now living it up in gay Paree. And here am I sitting next to a stranger, fat from boredom, with graying hair, sagging tits, spreading ass and all."

"Some men like big asses," I said. She smiled at me; my first reward. "You know," I continued, "your problem is that you're downgrading yourself because your husband left you."

"Well, of course. I mean, he wouldn't have left me if I were worth having, would he?"

"I don't go with that theory. When I was a young man, I had a wife. One day I walked in on her in bed with another man. I didn't think any the less of myself for—" I stopped my heart-piercing story when Susan fell into an enormous fit of giggles.

"What's so funny?" I asked.

"You walking in on your wife!" she managed to get out. "That must have been hysterical."

"Not at the time," I said coldly, picking up the plane's magazine from the pocket in front of me. That's what I get for trying to give emotional support.

Susan subsided in stages, especially after she saw she had hurt my feelings, a feat not easily accomplished.

"I'm sorry," she said tenderly, reaching over to grasp my hand. "I mean, well, it's a case of misery loving company, isn't it? Frankly, I don't see how any woman could leave you. Of course you are a bit too sure of yourself, but physically you're, um, stimulating."

"This morning you said I was a sagging he-man."

"I shouldn't have said that, should I?" she asked, leering at me. "After all, it's something that has to be checked out first."

Paris, a city of imposing edifices hiding a crumbling morality . . . We barely noticed it as my company car whisked us to my apartment overlooking the left bank. The maid had just had enough time to dust and to change the linens before Susan and I made our way to the top floor and into the apartment, depositing ourselves on the bed.

She was very Rubenesque, a definite change from my usual model-thin, bone-knocking blondes. It was like sinking into a soft pillow or tunneling my way through to mother earth. I lost myself in her body and only vaguely felt the pressure of her arms about me, demanding sexual reassurance.

We luxuriated on the puffed white sheets afterward, touching each other to give meaning to our hasty mating.

"You're definitely not sagging," she whispered to me.

How right she was.

We cuddled within each other, a prologue to beginning again. The sound of our exploding love echoed in my ears. Only the sound was too real. I kicked Susan off the bed and rolled on top of her as a Katyusha rocket shattered the living room of my apartment.

The doorbell rang. How inappropriate. I shoved Susan under the bed, opened the drawer of the bedside table and grabbed my automatic.

Shots were being fired from somewhere outside. Either they were poor shots or they weren't being aimed in my direction. I slid myself over to the bedroom window and looked out. Just in time to see a Renault try to roar off up the street. It never made it. More shots were fired. The car window shattered and the driver, injured or dead, slammed the car into the stone embankment, leaving his accomplice uncovered and soon to be dead as more shots rang out, hitting him, judging from his reflexes, right in the stomach. The Palestinian summit had obviously begun.

The doorbell continued to ring. Naked as I was, I decided to determine if it was friend or foe. It was Ali Gamel, my Egyptian counterpart. Not trusting him, I still held my automatic at the ready as I let him in.

"I see they fired too soon," he said coolly as he surveyed my demolished living room.

"You were their target?" I asked him doubtfully. After all, I was much more important than Ali.

"I assume so," he said. "I assume they were trying to stop this contact between us. Luckily my men were ready for them."

"You mean you were the cause of this total destruction of my property?"

"Obviously."

"Then your country damn well better fork over the money for the repairs."

"Don't be silly. Surely you have insurance to cover this."

"My insurance exempts war zones."

"But you're a rich man. What's a hundred thousand to you?"

I was about to explain my theory that every penny counts when we heard the clarion call of the Paris police. Ali calmly brushed aside the plaster from one of my Danish modern chairs and took out a cigarette. I hastened into the bedroom to slip on some clothes and to make sure Susan did the same.

Chapter 12

THE PARIS POLICE were rather beastly, but neither Ali nor I cared. After all, they invite this sort of thing by basing their foreign policy on ass-licking. I pointed this out to them and they were about to declare me persona non grata when I threatened to close down several of my French-based factories. They retreated from their position immediately. I think I had made my point.

Still, all was not sugar and spice. Fortunately Susan and I had not unpacked, so it was easy to transfer our luggage to another apartment of mine, on the right bank. Less fashionable, but acceptable under the circumstances. And I made Ali promise not to visit me there.

Then of course it was down to business. I told Ali I still hadn't heard from Tel Aviv. He found that unbelievable.

"What's the stall?" is the way he put it. Egyptians, like Israelis, are totally addicted to American movies.

"I just flew in from Rumania."

"I know, but you were at your embassy in Bucharest for quite some time."

"That was to give the information," I explained carefully. "I received nothing in return except the suggestion that I station myself in Paris, and here I am."

"I thought we were going to cooperate on this matter."

"And so we are," I said. "That's exactly why I am here. So we can cooperate. Right?"

"You Israelis. Your word is shit."

"Do you know they're trying to develop a new fuel from manure?"

"Then you'll be rich, won't you," he sneered.

So much for engaging his intellectual faculties.

"Well, what's the situation from your point of view?" I asked.

Ali hesitated and then plunged in. "The situation stinks. So far as we know, ten separate Palestinian organizations have already shown up. And their stay in Paris is not being financed by any oil-rich sheiks. The money is decidedly Red. We have it from a Syrian informant that Kolonikov is making his way to Paris in disguise to address this summit meeting. Tewfiq Hassani is also coming, to impress the Palestinians with the prowess of the Syrian military machine. Of interest to you is that he is bringing Syria's battle plans with him."

"Battle plans are always subject to change."

"They're worth having in any case."

"How true. Anything else?"

"No, my Israeli friend. And next time we meet, I hope you have some information you would like to exchange. Otherwise I might be forced to suggest to my government that we consider joining our Syrian and Palestinian brothers in another war."

"Don't do that, Ali. It's not healthy."

He twitched his lips and was gone.

I again made my weary way to the Israeli embassy, this time the Paris branch. Outside the embassy was a less than discreetly parked panel truck. Assuming that the French security service was inside, I smiled brightly and waved. No doubt they were pleased since under the most adverse circumstances I am still terribly photogenic.

At Israel's Paris embassy they knew me well. I merely nodded and made my way up to the second floor, where security was located. I went into the office expecting to see Ari Meir. Instead I saw Dan Tov.

After a few hugs and bear slaps, we got down to business.

"Like old times, eh?" Dan said as I sat down to relate all of Ali's information.

"So what do we have to give him?" I asked.

"A terror campaign against the Palestinian groups."

"He might not go for it. Arab against Arab and all that."

"Well, of course if you put it that way he won't go for it," Dan reprimanded me. "But we don't say Arab against Arab. We say Egyptian against Syrian, Egypt against the Black September, Egypt against the May Day Brigade, Egypt against Guerrillas for Galilee. See what I mean?"

"Yes."

"Now look: Ali was right. Ten Palestinian organizations have been invited to this summit. Unfortunately we have infiltrators in only four of the groups, so we can expect only limited information. But we all know what our course of action must be. We must disrupt this summit and if possible destroy any possibility of Palestinian unification.

"The only fair thing to do is to split this list down the middle. Of course we automatically take the four in which we have men, so we can protect them. Now, you give Ali his half of the list and tell him any action taken must be made to look as if it came from another Palestinian group, the Russians or the Syrians. And we have to act fast. According to our sources, the Palestine summit takes place in three days. If we can break the Palestinian coalition, we can stop the war. Syria won't go to war alone."

"Right," I said, taking the list. "I'll deliver it to Ali tonight. Right now I'm going to get a little rest."

"With Susan?" Dan asked.

"Do you have any other suggestions?"

He merely smiled.

When I opened the door to my apartment, Susan jumped up from a chair and came over to me. "My CIA contact just called," she said nervously. "He wants to know what you're doing."

"Well, tell him," I said, unzipping my pants and letting them fall to the floor.

To: Haim Zion, Minister of Defense
From: Dan Tov
Subject: Operation Paris Triangle

David met with Ali Gamel. The Palestinian, Syrian and Russian (Kolonikov) representatives are planning to have a summit conference in Paris in three days' time. Our immediate plan of action is to try to disrupt fraternal feelings between the Palestinian groups. We have split the ten groups equally between Egypt and ourselves. I am requesting permission to use the Flying Triangles for one evening.

So far reports from our men inside the Palestinian organizations show that while there is much vying for position, there is a general agreement that the time might be right for concerted action against the state of Israel. Here's hoping we can change their mind.

As far as your personal request to keep tabs on Susan Sasson, I can assure you that at the time of this writing she is probably in bed with David.

Though I realize that an insatiable curiosity is not always a bonus in this profession, I would like an answer to the following questions:

Is Susan Sasson really Susan Sasson?
Does her husband work for us?
Does her husband work for them?
Where is Jacob Sasson?
Why are you interested in Susan Sasson?

To: Dan Tov, Chief, Section 6–3
From: Haim Zion, Minister of Defense
Subject: Operation Paris Triangle

Keep up the good work.
Flying Triangles being sent to you at the expense of your department.

Re: Susan Sasson
 Mind your own business.

Chapter 13

I MET ALI that night and handed him his half of the list. Of course there was no way to stop him from concluding that we chose the groups in which we had men planted. But that was a problem for another day.

Now we had to get started on our disruptive campaign, which Ali had labeled Peanut Brittle. I couldn't figure it out either. Leaving him to his tasks, I put in a call to Dan Tov.

"Need any help?" I asked.

"Not tonight," he said. "I've called in the Flying Triangles."

Knowing then that the fate of Israel was in good hands, I returned to my dalliance with Susan.

"I told the CIA what you were doing," she said to me during a meal in one of Paris's most overrated restaurants. "They were very impressed—not that I went into details," she hastily assured me.

"Of course they were impressed," I said to her. "Americans generally vastly overinflate the intimacy of a love-making situation. I think that's because American men are definitely puerile."

"What do you mean? I feel very close to you when we're making love."

"And I feel close to you. But what do we talk about afterward? Certainly not anything that could be labeled top secret."

"Only romantically speaking."

"Of course. But the CIA probably suggested that you get me to talk in the afterglow about the current situation, of which I hope you know very little. They probably feel that I, like them, have a need to brag afterward, to make myself look more important than I am. Impossible."

She smiled at me. "So what shall I tell them?" she asked.

"Tell them nothing for the time being; keep them on a string. We might need them later."

We didn't get up till eleven the next morning, whereupon I opened the door and scooped up all the newspapers I had delivered to me. While I reviewed the *Wall Street Journal,* Susan took the International *Herald Tribune.*

"My God!" she said.

"What's the matter, more inflation?"

"Do you know last night five Palestinians were killed in their beds?"

"And it's in the paper already?" I asked. "Let me see that." I pried the paper away from her. It was the late edition and yes, five Palestinians were killed in their—

Susan grabbed the paper back. "The story says it looks like natural causes, each dying from a heart attack, but Paris police are suspicious. Here's more. All five were seen leaving various bars and cafés in the Algerian section of Paris with various well-endowed blondes. Police will continue their investigation."

I had another sip of coffee and returned to my stocks.

"David?"

"Yes," I said, turning the page of the newspaper.

"Is this the current situation you referred to last night?"

"For yourself or the CIA?" I asked.

"For myself."

"Then yes, it is."

"Well, what's happening?"

"The Palestinians are trying to put together a fighting coalition to attack Israel from Lebanon, and we are trying to stop them."

"Was this one of your efforts?"

"Yes."

"These women?"

"We call them our Flying Triangles. They're our sex squad."

"You mean they lured these Palestinians into bed and then . . ."

"Shot them with a hypodermic. Very effective too, I must say."

"That's awful."

"Why?"

"Women shouldn't kill."

"Oh, Susan."

"It's not right. Women are meant to give life, not take it away."

"And men are meant to kill?" I demanded of her.

"Yesterday you said American men were childish. Well, they're not the only ones. All men are children. They grab for what they want, and if they don't get it, they have a tantrum. Then they beat each other blind and limp home to their women, expecting to be embraced back into the comforting womb. It's not right to degrade women by using them to play your silly games."

"These women are Israeli women. They are strong like men."

"If they are so strong, then why do you use them as a sex squad? If they are so strong, why didn't they just attack these terrorists in some alley and strangle them instead of dangling their sexual apparatus as the main attraction?"

"What one cannot accomplish by force may be accomplished by stealth. Remember Judith? One of ours."

"Another homily from David the Wise?"

"Look, my pampered, middle-class American treasure, Israel is in a fight for its survival. We will use every means possible to win that fight and that includes cunts. Now would you like to go for a walk on this brilliant spring morning in Paris? We can walk over to the flower markets. I'll buy you a bouquet."

"And I'll shove it up my cunt so I can smell nice for you."

"Don't be crude, Susan. It doesn't become you. Leave the dishes in the sink. I'll do them later."

"How liberated of you."

The streets of Paris were rather gay that morning, and despite our moral antagonism, Susan cheered up considerably. And so did I when I saw the posters littering the Paris streets. The poster had no verbal message, just a picture of Arafat without kaffiyeh, dark glasses and growth.

"Who is the man?" Susan asked. "Is he running for something?"

"That's Arafat without his machismo," I answered.

"Really? I've never seen him like that. You know, he looks like Tweety Bird. A comic strip character," she informed me when she saw I didn't understand. "Did the Palestinians put them up?"

"No. I believe Dan Tov did, hoping probably to humiliate Arafat into leaving town."

After buying flowers, we took a short Metro ride to the Champs Élysées, where we made like tourists and sat in an expensive sidewalk café watching the people.

"The French do have a certain style," Susan said.

At the moment I couldn't agree with her, as I saw a schlemiel strolling down the boulevard. It was Dan Tov, not dressed for the kill. I signaled to him and he came over to join us.

"Why do you go around looking like that?" I asked him as I

sat in my neatly pressed Dacron polyester lightweight suit.

"It's all I brought with me," he answered, giving a nod of recognition to Susan.

"How's it going?" I asked.

Dan looked at Susan.

"It's okay. She caught on from this morning's paper."

"From our side, okay," he said. "You saw my posters, of course."

"Very effective."

"Ali has been busy too. Several car accidents, a few suicides."

"No man is an island, and all that."

"A more appropriate quote," Susan broke in, "would be 'never send to know for whom the bell tolls; it tolls for thee.' "

"Meaning?" Dan asked, annoyed.

"Meaning," Susan resumed, "if you kill off the leaders of these Palestinian groups, you are killing off the most conservative elements. Obviously they have a vested interest in keeping the situation the way it is, the Palestinian organizations split. With the old leaders out of the way, and in such suspicious circumstances, the young leaders might well forget their dogmas and unite in a common front against the enemy. The enemy, gentlemen, is you."

Unfortunately Susan's words proved entirely too prophetic. Despite Egypt's and Israel's best destructive capacities, the Palestinian representatives, those that were left, were going to have their summit after all.

To: Haim Zion, Minister of Defense
From: Dan Tov, Paris
Subject: Operation Paris Triangle

Unfortunately, although our operation was a success, it was a failure. Meaning the Palestinian summit takes place tonight. Don't worry. We have all fronts covered. Our men will be on the inside; their controls have been flown to Paris and are waiting to coordinate reports with the general picture.

David Haham and Ali Gamel are covering from the outside. We hope to be able to report the whole operation in Technicolor.

Susan Sasson remains with David.

Chapter 14

THE PALESTINIAN SUMMIT took place in a youth hostel outside the city limits. As a signal of recognition, all participants were to be riding Raleigh bicycles. One beneficial aspect of this was that it helped the British balance of payments. Another was that it enabled Ali and me to take perfect if sweaty pictures with our infrared cameras of all those arriving. Mohammed Sadeq, our Palestinian friend from Rumania, was one of the first to arrive, pedaling hard. After him the Palestinians came in groups of two or three. For some the bike could be classified as a foreign instrument of torture.

It was obvious after the first half hour of our stakeout that the plan was for the Palestinians to arrive first. Ali counted twenty arrivals; I counted twenty-one. Then there was a lull.

As Ali and I waited, wondering if our information was correct or if this were just a pre-summit conference of Palestinian groups alone, several of the terrorists came out of the hostel with guns. They were obviously posting guards. Two men were placed outside the main entrance, and two more started walking up the road a bit. They would probably station themselves along the road to keep outsiders definitely out.

Minutes followed, until Ali and I both spotted bicycle lights coming rather slowly down the road. We got our cameras ready.

It was Tewfiq Hassani, the Syrian, along with two aides. One of the aides carried in his bike basket a two-foot-square folder. We assumed this contained Syria's battle plans. Leaving their bikes outside—unlocked, I might add—they went in to join their blood brothers.

We waited again, but this time the interval was shorter. The lights we saw coming our way were accompanied by the quiet roar of a small motor. True to a classless society, Kolonikov was arriving at the summit chauffeured. This should have come as no surprise. Due to his bulk, bicycle riding would have been quite painful for him. Instead he was sitting in a small coolie-type carriage while two aides riding motorbikes attached to the carriage by ropes pulled him along. They stopped at the main entrance to the hostel but forgot to slow down enough first. Kolonikov's carriage smashed into the bikes and he was thrown out of it and into the dirt.

"One down and twenty-five to go," Ali said.

"Twenty-six," I corrected him.

He gave me an annoyed look as we turned our attention back to our wounded Russian. His aides were helping him up and brushing him off while he held his hands to his face. One aide took out a handkerchief and slowly pried Kolonikov's hands away. Through infrared glasses we could see blood dripping down Kolonikov's forehead and from his nose. After the aide had checked the flow from the forehead, he made Kolonikov lean his head back and applied a clean hanky to his nose. With head back and stomach thrust forward, Kolonikov entered the summit. After he was safely inside, the Palestinian guards looked at each other and shook their heads.

Now was our time to move. Ali and I had reviewed a plan of the hostel before we set out on our night's vigil, so we knew where we were going. Besides the main entrance, the hostel had a back door and a series of windows on either side. We had decided to split up. Ali would take the left bank of windows, I the right. This way, if either of us was spotted, the other had a chance of escaping with whatever information had so far been collected.

Ali's side was easier to get to, as we were already on the left. I decided that instead of taking the chance of crossing the road, I would accompany Ali to his windows, then cross around in back. Our plan was to meet at our original station when the meeting had broken up.

After seeing Ali in position, I circled around through the brush, amazed to see no guard posted at the back door. Amazed but grateful. It made it all the easier for me to get to my side.

Once along the right window banks, I noticed that the windows were half opened. This was good and bad. Good because I could hear them; bad because they could hear me. I lifted my head slightly and saw why the back door hadn't been guarded without. It was guarded from within. Three armed guards—one Russian, one Syrian, one Palestinian. They were not only guarding the door, they were guarding their men. In front of the guards was a table with three chairs. One for Kolonikov, one for Mohammed Sadeq, and the third for Tewfiq Hassani. To their sides sat their aides. Looking toward them for guidance were the twenty-odd Palestinians that had gathered at the hostel. Kolonikov's bleeding seemed to have stopped. His head was upright, though he still held the handkerchief to his nose. Mohammed Sadeq was talking.

"So, fellow Palestinians, we few are left. After the dastardly efforts by the Israelis and even our brothers from Egypt—" Shouts of "No! No!" arose from the floor. "Yes, it is true. After their efforts to kill us off, we remain as we were before, strong, virile, and ready to retake our homeland."

This brought cheers from his audience.

"This time," he continued, "we shall succeed. This time, with the help of our Russian brothers, our Syrian brothers, and yes, even those faithless Egyptian women, we shall slay the Jews and return our land to our people." More cheers for Mohammed. "Now," he said, "I turn the platform over to Tewfiq Hassani, our faithful friend and supporter for many years. He will show us the plan of battle."

Tewfiq stood up and took center stage. He snapped at his aide with the folder and the aide promptly hung the battle plan from the back wall. I got my camera ready. At the first outburst of further enthusiasm, I would photograph the map.

"Here," he began, "are Syria, Lebanon, the Sinai and the usurper state of Israel. Here, here and here are the main concentrations of troops along our borders with Israel. Here and here are our main bases from which an attack by air will be launched. Here, this base near Buraq, is your air base. I say yours because there will be fifty MIG's stationed at this base to protect your armies as you cross into your homelands."

"We have no pilots," someone shouted.

"Yes, you do," Tewfiq said, smiling. "You have the voluntary expeditionary force from Russia."

"Da, da." Kolonikov nodded.

"Your troops should be placed here," Tewfiq continued, "along Fatahland, two miles removed from the Lebanese-Israeli border. As I understand it, the consensus is that each Palestinian group will be under the generalship of its own leader, who will then coordinate battle plans with Mohammed Sadeq."

As they voiced their agreement, I took my picture.

"Now," Tewfiq said as he sat down, "let's open the floor to questions."

"How will Egypt come in?"

"Egypt," Tewfiq assured the questioner, "will have to come in to save face. It is either that or be laughed out of the Arab League. She cannot play the old woman forever. Besides, when she sees how well the fighting is going, she will want to come in to regain her territory."

"How about Jordan?"

Mohammed Sadeq answered this one. "Jordan, as you know, has not been very forthcoming regarding cooperation with its Palestinian brothers, fearing, quite rightly, that we plan to assassinate the king." Chuckles from his audience, more pictures from me. "Still, once we have overrun Israel, we will turn our knife's edge toward Amman. Until then we must be patient. We cannot station troops on the Jordanian border."

"How well will we be protected? Even with the MIG's, the Israelis are bound to bombard us."

"Are you men or dogs!" Kolonikov exploded. "When we were in Stalingrad, we did not ask these questions," he yelled, pounding on the table. "If you want your land, take it. Stop sniveling like women."

A hostile murmur arose from the crowd. Knives were drawn. Russian tact had struck again.

Tewfiq stood up to save the day. "Thank you for those spirited words, Comrade Kolon—nikov," he added belatedly. "What our Russian brother means is that the Union of Soviet Socialist Republics, all democratic states combined to fight imperialism—"

"Da, da," Kolonikov interrupted.

"—has generously bestowed on Syria a new weapon that will wipe out Israeli air power."

"Like what?" someone shouted.

"Like a laser-guided missile."

"Laser like in that James Bond movie, splitting up the metal toward his crotch?"

"Exactly," Tewfiq lied.

A murmur of approval swept the hall. "We are ready!" they shouted, and "Palestine liberated, Palestine! Palestine! Palestine!"

"When?" someone intelligently called out.

Kolonikov stood grandly up. "Right now," he pronounced, "our ships are carrying these magical weapons through the Dodecanese straits. In two days' time they will be unloaded at the Syrian port of Latakia. Four days later they will be in position. In two weeks from today war will break out in the Middle East. Gather your men along the borders now! The day of the Jew has ended in Palestine!"

Shouts of joy broke out among the Palestinians. Kolonikov had risen to the occasion.

As the meeting began to break up, Ali and I made our way back to our first station under cover of the noise of departure. Both of us were depressed.

"I think Egypt has picked the losing side," he said, looking pointedly at me.

"We've never lost yet," I assured him.

"Seventy-three?"

"Don't tell me you're beginning to believe your own lies about the Third Army?"

"We did make the crossing."

"Don't give yourself credit for that. It was our own incompetence. Anyway, enough of this. I have a decidedly devilish urge to get even with Kolonikov."

"If we touch him, the Russians will be down on us like a pack of dogs."

"Very apt description."

"And we will have a needless vendetta on our hands," Ali concluded sensibly.

"Why us?" I countered. "What if we deliver him to the CIA?"

Ali smiled in agreement. We took out our map and checked the lay of the land. It all depended on which direction Kolonikov was going. We stood up and began making our way to the crossroads, where we had hidden our car. We got in it and waited. Already from our vantage point we could see the bicycle set spread out down the various highways. Soon we were rewarded by the hum of a motor and the sight of Kolonikov's carriage. He was being pulled to the right, back to Paris.

Slowly Ali eased our car onto the road and we followed Kolonikov for some distance with our lights off. We couldn't run

90

Kolonikov down a hill; the land was flat. But we came up with a better plan. As soon as the road was totally deserted, Ali pulled on his lights and roared up behind Kolonikov.

They knew what was happening, but there was nothing they could do to stop it. Ali pulled from behind to diagonally in front of them, coming to a quick halt. As expected, they came to a rather critical stop themselves, smashing against the right side of our Citroën. Kolonikov flew out of the carriage, over the car, landing on his head again, not five feet from our door. I leaped out of the back seat and dragged him into the car. Barely waiting for me to pull Kolonikov's feet in, Ali took off down the road for Paris. He pulled up at the first public telephone and I jumped out, got the chief CIA control in Paris and told him, in my best Texas accent, where we would leave Kolonikov. Before he could utter a goddamn-who-is-this, I hung up.

Ali parked the Citroën at the appropriate place. We got our equipment from the car, taped and wrapped Kolonikov, and then took off.

Reaching a truck stop, we found a vegetable truck headed for the Paris markets. We climbed under the tarpaulin and bragged of our adventures on our way into town. As the truck slowed to a stop, we hopped off.

Ali said, "What now?"

"Now," I said to him, "it's up to us."

"Good luck," he said to me, taking my hand. "Remember, we don't want this war, but if it comes, we'll have to join in."

"Shalom."

"Salaam."

Transmission 10–20
From: Agent H-7
To: Nassem Nasri, Chief, Section 8–2

Lenin and Trotsky dead!
Lenin and Trotsky dead!
Shot near border trying to escape.
No way to help.
Clear out of Phoenicia. Now!
Repeat:
Lenin and Trotsky dead!

To: Haim Zion, Minister of Defense
From: Nassem Nasri, Chief, Section 8–2
Subject: Phoenician Contact

Regret to inform you Lenin and Trotsky dead. Shot near border trying to escape.
Please send appropriate contact to inform Trotsky's family.
No hope for return of body.
No reason to believe so far Trotsky recognized as ours.
Suggest immediate evacuation of Phoenicia.

To: Tuvia Bloomburg, Chief, Section 4–4
From: Haim Zion, Minister of Defense
Subject: Yuri Greenglass

With greatest regrets must inform you that Yuri Greenglass was killed along the Syrian border a few hours ago.
Please inform his family and let me know their condition. I understand he had two sons. I will pay them a visit tomorrow, not that it will help.
Take immediate steps to close down his operations in your sector until you can ascertain the damage.
Sorry, Tuvia. He was too good to lose.

To: Natie Lev, Chief, Section 7–1
From: Haim Zion, Minister of Defense
Subject: Operation Phoenician Contact

Inform your agents that Operation Phoenician Contact is at an end. They are to clear out immediately.
Send message reading:
Trotsky, Lenin dead at border. Clear out. Make haste intelligently.

Transmission 10–31
To: Agent B-7
From: Natie Lev

Trotsky, Lenin dead at border. Clear out. Make haste intelligently.

Chapter 15

USING THE METRO, I made my way once again to the Israeli embassy and Dan's office. There was already quite a gathering as other agents at the summit reported by phone to their controls, who were littering the office. I handed my film to the developer and sat down to await the general meeting.

Everyone reported. We all had about the same thing to say. I neglected to mention Kolonikov's misfortune. The fewer who knew about it, the better, from my point of view. I would tell Dan later. After the film was developed, Syria's battle map was flashed on the wall. It wasn't much different from what we had known before. But then that gave very little comfort. Dan ordered the film sent by courier to the Israeli general staff immediately.

After the meeting broke up, Dan and I sat around his desk with our feet up, thinking our separate discouraging thoughts.

"You know there is going to be a war, don't you?" he said.

"No."

"What do you mean, no. You have any brilliant strategy in mind?"

"We have six days before the missiles are in place."

"Whoopee!"

"During those six days Israel must launch a preemptive strike against the Palestinians in Lebanon, the sooner the better. Destroy them. Wipe them out. That's the answer."

"What's to stop Syria from coming in a few days sooner? They still have their old missile protection system."

"The Syrians don't think that fast, and furthermore the Russians won't allow it. If the Russian ships dock in two days at Latakia, the missiles and laser devices are going to be on Syrian soil. If Syria launched a joint attack before the missiles were in place, Israel could simply wipe the missiles out of existence before they were operational. Russia won't let that happen. A preemptive strike against the Palestinians. That's the only hope now."

"I'll pass your word down to the lesser creatures on the general staff," Dan said.

"You won't have to," I assured him. "They'll think of it themselves. It's the only way. But you might suggest the third day."

"Third?"

"Yes. The whole maneuver for war will be at its most vulnerable on that day. The missile systems will be off the boats and traveling across Syria far from their destinations. The Palestinians should be grouped in southern Lebanon, but far from organized. Yes, the third day should be perfect."

"I'll pass it along," Dan said.

"And hard," I said. "Hit them hard so there's no chance of a military comeback in the near future."

"It will buy us time."

"Yes, time to see our sons grow up and fall in some other battle."

"Yes," Dan agreed sadly. "It's true. But it is worth fighting for, worth dying for. Our land."

"Unfortunately the Palestinians think the same."

We got up and left the office, locking it behind us. Dan would fly back to Israel on the first plane tomorrow and I thought I would join him. I used to enjoy traveling but now I enjoyed more being at home.

"Yoohoo. Mar Tov!" the communications secretary yelled at Dan from down the hall.

We turned around and waited for her approach.

"I have a telephone message to give to you," she said when she finally caught up with us. "It's for a Mr. Dan Tov," she read, "to pass along to Mr. David Haham."

"I'm David Haham," I said. "What's the message?"

"It's from a Mrs. Susan Sasson. S-a-s-s-o-n," she spelled, looking up for applause. She was obviously a relative of the communications minister. She couldn't have gotten to Paris on merit alone.

"Very well done," I said. "Is there any message or did she just leave her name?"

"Oh, no! There's a message and I think it is a very important one."

"May I see it?"

She stepped back in case I was going to grab the message from her hand. Then she read it. "David, I have spotted my husband and am following him. He went to Orly with his bimbo, b-i-m-b-o, and is about to take an Air France flight to Beirut. I must follow him and find out why. Susan."

"May I have the message?" I asked.

She handed me the slip of paper while Dan uttered a pointed good night to her.

"I was right," Dan said to me, dragging me over to the wall.

"You were right, what?"

"He is involved."

"Involved in what?"

"Involved in this whole thing. I knew it. Once I catch the smell of the hunt, I'm never far off."

"You thought he had invented a ray gun."

"Ray gun, laser-guided missile. They're all the same."

"Well, I can't believe it."

"Why not?"

"I don't know," I said. "Something is wrong. But I don't believe it has anything to do with our problem."

"It could have."

"I'm worried about Susan. Especially in Beirut at this time. She has children, you know."

"I know and I understand," Dan said. "There's only one thing for you to do."

"What?"

"Go to Beirut."

"Beirut! Are you kidding? You've got to be out of your mind. They'd recognize me in a minute."

"Don't flatter yourself, David. It's been years."

"It's been years, but they know me. And now with all this happening in the south of their country, they are going to be doubly careful."

"I never figured you for a coward, David."

"See how wrong you can be about someone?"

"Susan Sasson," he said, clicking his tongue. "That name's so Jewish, they'll probably pick her up even though she has an American passport. Of course her husband is probably using a phony Russian one."

"Cut it, Dan."

He stood back and looked at me. "Yes, yes," he said, sizing me up. "Some gray hair, a mustache and beard. A little cotton in the cheeks. Let's go," he said, pulling me down the hallway, back to his office.

He called his crew in and they went to work on me. My hair was turned gray, a beard and mustache added, streaked with gray. Then cotton was put in my mouth. I felt my mouth ooze as the saliva soaked into the cotton. Then my picture was taken. Meanwhile Dan had dragged a cot into the room.

"Lie down here," he said. "Get some rest. You're going to need it. But don't mess the hair."

They all left the room and I lay down to sleep. I didn't know if I would go through with this. I was worried about Susan, but I was also worried about myself. The Lebanese knew me and I was fair game. That less than comforting thought accounted for the nightmares that followed.

Dan came in the morning with a suitcase full of unfashionable clothing for me. While I changed, he gave me my French passport, an American passport with my true facial characteristics, French money, Lebanese money and my cover story: French businessman going on holiday to Beirut to visit the banks.

One of the embassy drivers took me from the embassy grounds out into Paris traffic, where we drove around for half an hour making sure we lost anyone who might happen to have tailed us. Then we headed for the airport. I checked in at Air France and waited for my flight to Beirut. While I read the morning paper, I saw Dan Tov making his way past the El Al gates on his way back to Israel. I cursed him from the bottom of my being.

To: Haim Zion, Minister of Defense
From: Dan Tov, Paris
Subject: Operation Paris Triangle

Following are the various reports from the operation in Paris. As you can see, they all concern the Palestinian summit. Attached also are photos of participants and battle maps. David took them. It should be obvious that the situation does not look promising. I would recommend a partial call-up immediately.

David, after reviewing the situation, suggested that in three days the Israel army stage a preemptive strike against the Palestinians in southern Lebanon. I am inclined to agree with his assessment. Syria will be caught off guard, the Russians won't want to lose their new missiles, and Egypt doesn't want war in the first place, so they say. I'll be available to discuss this with you later in the day. I am sending this communiqué from Paris, but I expect to be home a few hours after your receipt of this.

Concerning the other situation, the one with Susan Sasson, there have been new developments. She spotted her husband in Paris with another woman and followed them to Beirut. I am convinced that her husband, Jacob Sasson, is in some way involved in this whole mess. I have persuaded David to fly to Beirut and get to the bottom of this matter.

To: Haim Zion, Minister of Defense
From: Miriam Halevi, Paris Embassy
Subject: Operation Phoenician Contact

Got your message and acted on it with much regret. What went wrong? I flew from Beirut last night, as we all figured that my credentials, being French, were much less reliable than J.S.'s, with his American passport.

B-7 has once again faded into the woodwork. She feels she is safe.

J.S. is staying overnight at his hotel and flying on the afternoon plane to Paris and New York. I will station myself at Orly to make sure of his safe arrival and departure.

He showed me a very interesting time, which I can show you as I have it in blushing Technicolor. He seems to feel that his wife would definitely object to adultery, so you have something on him in the future if you need it. To me he seemed to be acceptably committed, besides having a good set of teeth.

Love,
Miri

To: Dan Tov, Paris
From: Haim Zion, Minister of Defense
Subject: David Haham, Susan Sasson

Idiot! Recall Haham immediately!

Rewire to Tel Aviv, please.
Ari Meir

To: Haim Zion, Minister of Defense
From: Dan Tov, Tel Aviv
Subject: David Haham

"Idiot." Why? I can't recall Haham. He's already in Beirut. I never knew you were that close to him. But don't worry. He can take care of himself. Take a tranquilizer and count from one hundred to one. It always works for me.

To: Rafi Golum, Chief of Staff
From: Haim Zion, Minister of Defense
Subject: Operation Bloody September

Now that you have been totally informed of the situation and have had time to consult with the senior staff, what are your options?

I think David's idea is the best. In three days' time the whole operation will be most vulnerable from their side. Prepare a plan of action based on Haham's idea and bring the details to me as soon as possible. That means within the next four hours.

To: Haim Zion, Minister of Defense
From: Rafi Golum, Chief of Staff
Subject: Operation Bloody September

Dear Haim,

I am preparing as you suggested a battle strategy for the imminent attack on Palestinian encampments in southern Lebanon.

There is one small point I would like to clear up. This strategy is based on the combined intelligence of my entire senior staff and has absolutely no relationship to the suggestions of David Haham, who as you know is not even a member of the military. I feel strongly that this point be noted. Let's give credit where credit is due.

With growing respect,
Rafi

To: Dan Tov, Chief, Section 6–3
From: Rafi Golum, Chief of Staff
Subject: David Haham

When I need David's advice, I'll ask for it. Until then he can buttoutski.

★ III ★
The Middle East

Chapter 16

BEIRUT WAS A MARKETPLACE. And in the marketplace you could buy anything. It was my sort of town.

No trouble getting through passport control. No trouble getting into town. Trouble finding Susan. I sat in my hotel room overlooking the Mediterranean and put calls through the desk one after another to all the first-class hotels, asking if they had a Susan Sasson registered. No, none of them did. I tried the second-class hotels. Fifth down on the list, the Aladdin. Yes, a Mrs. Susan Sasson was registered, but she was out now. Yes, she had taken full board. It was cheaper. Yes, they expected her back for lunch.

Thanking them, I hung up. Now I had to move fast. No one in Beirut was going to sit in his hotel room calling other hotels and asking for a Jewish woman without arousing some suspicion. I had to get out of there as quickly as possible before some diligent hotel employee contacted the police.

I took a quick shower, getting the gray out of my hair and removing my mustache and beard. Then I dressed in a white shirt and ill-fitting trousers, the only ones that came with my role of French businessman. Taking my money, but leaving the now unnecessary French passport, I slipped out of my room, made my way by elevator to the second floor, then walked down the stairs to the lobby, going out a side entrance onto the street.

The Aladdin on Rue Minet al-Husn was also along the Mediterranean, though farther down the avenue, where the hotels became less conspicuously luxurious.

I waited for an hour at a conveniently located café until I saw Susan coming up the sidewalk, making her way back to the hotel for lunch.

I crossed the street swiftly and got there before she came to the hotel entrance. I took her from behind by the arm. Startled, she turned quickly.

"You," she said. "You scared me. You shouldn't be here, you know. They'll kill you if they find you."

"Any other pleasant words of welcome?"

"Oh, David, I am glad to see you. I don't know what I should do."

"Come on. Let's take a walk and talk about it."

"But I'll miss my lunch. I've already paid for it."

"I'll buy you lunch so you won't lose out on anything."

"Well, all right."

We walked for a while until we came to a café clean enough for Susan's tastes. After we ordered shashlik, Susan told me what had been happening to her.

"He's alone now."

"Jacob?"

"Yes," she said. "He came with this woman, unfortunately very good-looking. They checked into the Desert Inn together and then went to the Paradice Hotel."

"And he came out alone?"

"Yes. I don't understand it. I went to the Desert Inn this morning and asked if Mr. Sasson was still in his room. The clerk said yes and that he asked not to be disturbed. Jacob didn't come out all morning."

"That could mean a number of things," I said, "none of them particularly good."

"So what should we do?" she asked.

"Go back to the Desert Inn and find out if your husband is still there."

Just then the waiter brought the food. I paid him for the meal, put the shashlik inside the pita and gave one to Susan, keeping the other for myself.

"Oh, good," she said. "I love sandwiches better than eating off a plate."

"It's the primitive in you."

We ate our way back down the avenue to the Desert Inn.

"What room number?" I asked her as we entered the hotel lobby.

"I never asked."

I ambled over to the desk and asked, "Do you have a Jacob Sasson registered here?"

"Yes," the clerk, a young boy, said. "You just might be able to catch him. He's checking out for a flight back to New York. Room 503."

Susan and I just looked at each other as we zoomed upward in the elevator.

When we got into the hallway, she said, "Are you sure this is the right thing to do?"

"Sure? At this point I am sure of absolutely nothing."

I knocked on Room 503. The door was opened by a man a few years younger than I, five inches shorter, but just as thin. He had dark skin, black hair, intelligent eyes and good teeth.

"Jacob Sasson?" I asked.

"Yes," he said impatiently.

I stepped aside to let Susan enter first.

"Susan!" he whispered hoarsely. "What in God's name are you doing here?"

"Oh, I just thought I'd take a nice little spring vacation and Beirut looked appealing in the travel brochures," she said, civilly enough.

Jacob still stood there in astonishment. Meanwhile I shoved Susan farther inside the room and closed the door.

Noticing me again, Jacob pulled Susan behind him to protect her and asked, "Who are you?"

"He's okay," Susan began. "I met—"

"Susan, that's enough," I stopped her. To Jacob I said, "My name is David. I am like you."

"From Iraq?" he questioned.

"Yes."

"From Haaretz?"

"That too."

"It's true, Jacob. That's where I met him. Your nephew brought me to him. Ever since then he has been helping me find you."

"Now that we have found you," I said, "perhaps you would like to tell us what you are doing here in Beirut, in an Arab land?"

"Yes," Susan agreed.

"Can I assume that since you're Israeli and you are also in Lebanon, you have something to do with Israeli intelligence?"

"Something, yes. I used to work for them. And it seems as though I am doing so again."

"Well," he said, "I'll trust you. Not that I have much of a choice. You hold my life in your hands as it is."

"And you hold mine," I assured him.

He sat on the bed. Susan sat down next to him, holding his hand. "Two weeks ago," he began. "Was it only two weeks? Good God. Anyway, two weeks ago I was approached by Simcha Feistovitz. Do you know him?"

"Yes. Feistovitz. He works for Israel Aircraft Industries."

"Yes. He specializes in missiles, construction and counter-measures. Anyway, he came to Ann Arbor, invited himself, actually, to give a seminar to our department. I'm in aerospace engineering, you know."

"Yes, Susan told me."

"Then perhaps she told you that I also work in the missile field."

"Yes."

"Well, then, this will be easier for you to understand. After the seminar Feistovitz sought me out, wanted to go out for something to eat. I invited him home for dinner, but he begged off, saying he had to fly out immediately for Chicago.

"So we left the engineering quadrangle and were crossing the street for Miller's—Feistovitz wanted some American ice cream, said he really missed that in Israel—when a car pulled up and someone inside called out to him. ·

" 'Let's join Uri,' Feistovitz said. I had no objection. We climbed into the car and took off away from the campus area. Then Feistovitz put his proposal to me. It seems that a top Soviet scientist, Jewish by birth, though not by much else, had contacted one of Israel's agents in Moscow with some story about Russia's developing a laser-guided missile system which was operational and in the process of being loaded on ships headed for Syria and eventual use against Israel. The Russian scientist suggested to the Israeli agent that he could make copies of the laser's design and trade them for his freedom. You see, the Russian scientist was afraid to declare his desire to emigrate to Israel for various reasons, the main one being that he knew he would be killed if he mentioned it since he was working on the laser project.

"The Israeli agent relayed this information to his superior, who was definitely interested, though puzzled as to how he would get the scientist out of Russia. The Russians solved that problem for Israel. They were sending the scientist to Syria to supervise the setting up of the missile system. The Israelis promised the scientist that if he came across with the plans for the laser guidance system, they would come across with his freedom.

"The Israeli plan was simple. They would smuggle him from Syria into Lebanon. That's where I came into the arrangement. You see, my field is guidance and control. It's a limited field, where Feistovitz deals in generalities. The Israelis needed me to check on the plans that the Russian scientist brought with him to see if they were valid. I had worked in the field so I would know what to look for. Also I had an American passport so I would have no trouble getting into Lebanon. I didn't really want to cooperate, but the way Feistovitz put it to me was 'Do you want to be a part of Israel's destruction or Israel's salvation?' What could I say?

"Feistovitz told me I would receive a phone call, a woman's voice asking me if I had seen the movie *The Russians Are Coming, The Russians Are Coming.* That would be my signal. I would take off for New York, where I would meet my contact. So I flew to New York, but there was some holdup with the Russian side of it. We waited a few days there and then flew on to Paris. We stayed in a hotel in Paris until we got the go-ahead from Beirut. We flew here yesterday and went to the Paradice Hotel, where we were supposed to wait for the Russian scientist to make his appearance. We got word late last night that he wouldn't be coming. The Russians caught him and the Israeli agent near the Syrian border. They were both executed on the spot.

"Miriam, my contact, suggested I not make a move for the airport, but wait until midday today. It would be less suspicious. Then she and the other agent at the Paradice disappeared. I returned to the Desert Inn alone and was just getting ready to check out. Then you came."

"Oh, Jacob," Susan said, hugging him to her. "How awful for you."

"I know," he agreed.

"But why didn't you tell me anything? Didn't you know how worried I would be?"

"Yes, but they said three days. That's all. Three days and then I would be back with you. They would have arranged a fake auto accident and a doctor's certificate saying I had suffered a temporary lapse of memory due to the accident."

"And all this time I thought the whole thing had to do with your friend in Argentina or that postcard from Rumania."

"What?"

"You know, the friend who didn't get your New Year's card? That weird postcard from Rumania?"

"Yes, strange, but what possible connection could they have with this?"

"I don't know," Susan said. "I didn't know. I used any scrap of evidence I had to try to figure out what had happened to you. At least I was right in one thing," she said to me. "He was an Israeli spy."

"Yes," I said, wondering why Dan Tov had not known about it.

"Did you know about this all the time, David?" she asked.

"I'm as surprised about it as you are," I assured her.

"No one was to know," Jacob said. "Not even if you had connections within the intelligence community. Miriam told me that only she, I, this agent at the Paradice, the agent in Syria, and the Minister of Defense knew the actual plan. It was of top importance so it was kept top secret."

"Miriam?" Susan became alert, like a hound dog sniffing. "The woman in Paris? The good-looking one holding on to your arm in the airport?"

"My contact," Jacob said, blushing.

It was obvious from the silence in the room which accompanied Jacob's racing sweat glands that his contact with Miriam had been intimate. How would Susan handle it? If she had a screaming fit, she would attract all kinds of attention from the hotel staff, affecting our low profile. If she retaliated against

Jacob by pointing out that while he was on top of Miriam, she was under me, we would have more trouble. Jacob was an Iraqi, and no matter how civilized Iraqis seem on the surface, to us adultery is emotionally at least a killing offense. Bad blood between the three of us now, in Lebanon, could mean our deaths or, worse, our capture.

Susan considered the alternatives for a moment, her eyes focused on the pattern of the carpet. Finally she walked stiffly to the window overlooking the Mediterranean. She looked very English.

"Let's consider this your little fling, shall we, Jacob? In the same circumstances, I might have done the same thing."

Jacob stumbled over to her, kneeling beside her, kissing the hem of her skirt. She placed her hand on his ruffled hair, turned, and gave me a wicked little grin.

I couldn't resist. I began reciting: " 'Who can find a virtuous woman? For her price is far above rubies. The heart of her husband doth safely trust in her, so that he shall have no need of spoil. She will do him good and not evil all the days of her life.' "

Jacob finished the recital in Hebrew while Susan nobly accepted her due.

I gave them a few moments of precious silence before I said, "If you're packed, Jacob, perhaps we can check out of the hotel, pick up Susan's things and make it to the airport. During the flight to Europe we can discuss hiring a good marriage counselor."

Susan helped him up and together we struggled emotionally to the elevator, making our way down to the lobby. Then Susan and I waited on the side while Jacob checked out.

"Why didn't you tell him?" I asked, smiling gently at her.

"There's another proverb," she said, "the fourteenth, I believe: 'Every wise woman buildeth her house: but the foolish plucketh it down with her hands.' I may not be very bright, but I am not all that foolish."

"My compliments."

Jacob came over to us. We made our exit from the hotel and headed quickly down the avenue toward the Aladdin. Half a block away I saw three cars pull up in front of Susan's hotel. Several men jumped out. One of them was Suleiman Sallah, known to Israeli intelligence as Suleiman the Magnificent, the head of Lebanon's counterintelligence unit. He and his henchmen entered the Aladdin. We were too late. They were on our trail.

Chapter 17

I PULLED JACOB and Susan back gently from our intended destination. Susan gave me an annoyed look, but when she saw my face, she followed my direction without any trouble whatsoever. We took the first corner we found and headed down its sidewalk at too brisk a pace by Lebanese standards. Crisscrossing various streets put us in another section of Beirut, far enough from the luxurious tourist spots along the Mediterranean but not far enough so that our English would seem foreign and therefore suspicious. We sat down at a sidewalk café.

"What's happening?" Susan whispered, by now used to these sudden turns of events.

"I saw Suleiman Sallah, Lebanese intelligence, entering your hotel, and if I'm not mistaken, it's you he's after."

"Why?"

"It's all my fault. Sloppy work again. But I thought we could make it out of Lebanon in time."

She looked at me with a puzzled expression.

"You see, I called you from my hotel. I made too many calls asking for you. They must have checked my hotel room first and found I had left my clothes and a French passport. A stupid thing to do, but I didn't realize they would work so fast. They must really be on the alert. Then they came looking for you."

"So what would they do if they found me?" she asked.

"I don't know. They'd question you, and you know far too much for your own good. You know me, for one thing. You saw what went on in Paris. And now you know Jacob's story. There's too much you can tell them, and they won't believe you're not involved in any of this."

"Involved in what? She certainly wasn't involved with me," Jacob said.

Susan opened her mouth to tell him about Paris and the Palestinians, but I cautioned her, "Don't tell him. The less he knows, the safer he is. Matter of fact, right now, Jacob, you are the safest one here. The sooner you get out of Lebanon, the better. I'm finding a taxi right now and putting you in it."

"Don't bother," he said. "Do you think I'm going to leave Lebanon and leave Susan behind?"

"It's not a question of marital strategies now; it's a question of survival. No one's on to you. It's simply a question of picking yourself up, getting yourself to the airport, and flying out. And you'd better do it now before they pick up your trail from Susan's."

"What kind of man do you think I am, to leave Lebanon with my wife in danger? We either go or we stay, together."

"Perhaps you're making too much of this, David," Susan said. "After all, the Lebanese wouldn't mistreat an American citizen, and I do have an American passport."

"So do I," I answered.

"Oh."

"Look, the way I see it now, the only solution for you, Susan, is to make your way quickly to the American embassy. Find their security officer."

"How?"

"Just ask for one of the commercial attachés and if they give you any trouble, start screaming, 'CIA! CIA!' That'll get you action. When you make contact, tell him how you've been operating for the CIA in Rumania and Paris. Mention that guy's name. What was it, Bill O'Brian? They'll check it out, and when they verify it, chances are they'll give you a new identity and send you out of Lebanon by plane also. Both of you can then meet in New York."

"And what will you do?" Susan asked.

"I don't know," I said.

"Don't you know anyone here?"

"No one I trust. I haven't worked Lebanon for years."

"Well, I'm not leaving you here alone."

"Don't be ridiculous, Susan. I've spent a lifetime living by my wits. I'll be okay."

"We either all have a plan to get out safely or none of us goes," Jacob insisted.

"Easier said than done."

"Well"—Susan grew enthusiastic—"why don't we slip out over the border?"

"Which border did you want to slip through?" I asked. "Syria's to the north and west."

"But Israel's to the south."

"We can't go south. There's going to be a war there. Even now the Palestinians are gathering their forces. Fatahland will be closed to tourists."

"There's going to be another war?" Jacob asked, concerned.

"Always another war," I reminded him. "This time the Palestinians are fighting alongside the Syrians. And the Syrians are fighting because as you already know, the Russians are supplying them with laser-guided missiles."

"So they say," Jacob said. "But how effective are these missiles?"

"I've got to believe they're effective enough. The Russians will dock at Latakia with them tomorrow."

"I still would like to see the plans for that laser system. I

116

would like to know how they did it. How did they solve the engineering problems involved?"

"How the hell do I know? I don't know anything scientific about them. What are the problems involved?"

Jacob began his lecture. "Well, if you're really interested, the main problem with a laser is how can such a narrow beam lock onto the plane and stick with it in order to guide the missile. Are they using a conventional radar system to first pick up the plane?"

"I don't have any idea."

"It's a fantastic scientific advance," Jacob repeated, "if they actually accomplished it. I would really like to get my hands on one of those."

"Well, it's probably the size of a tank," I said.

"Oh, no," he disagreed. "It would only be about the size of a large box, enough to contain the laser beam and the sensor."

I sat up. "How large a box?"

"A large box. Like—like, say, the box a small refrigerator comes in."

"So not too large for a small truck, such as a pickup."

"Oh, you'd have ample room," he assured me.

"What could you learn if you by some chance captured one of these devices? Could you learn to outwit it?"

"Outwit it? Yes, you could. My main interest would be to see what kind of modulator they used for the beam and what kind of coding was used to help the missile track the airplane for interception. But I suppose you're looking at it more from the point of an air force outwitting the laser guidance system?"

"Yes."

"Well, the best way to outwit it would be to fly on a cloudy day."

"Why?"

"Since laser is a light beam, it only works on a clear day. It guides itself in one respect by the reflection from the target it is beaming to. To confuse this beam, which would then confuse the missile, you would have to perhaps outfit the plane with reflectors that would misrepresent the true position of the plane, therefore sending the missile on a harmless course. Or you could send in dummy planes with light sources that imitate the laser reflection itself, also leading to confusion and misguidance of any missile system based on the laser."

"So there are steps that could be taken to counteract this laser?"

"Of course. There is no such thing as the perfect weapon. Thank God. Unless of course you're planning to bomb everything out of existence. But then you might be faced with a mutant strain of human beings resistant to radiation."

"But now," I said, "I'd rather talk about the laser."

"So would I. What do you want to talk about?"

"To get a Russian laser system would be helpful to the West?"

"Certainly. Without a doubt."

"Do you speak Arabic?"

"Yes. But Iraqi dialect."

"Are you willing to come to Syria with me to pick one up?"

"One what?"

"One laser."

"You're crazy!" That was his immediate reaction.

"If it's as small as you say it is, why am I so crazy?"

"Because it's not something you just go into a store and buy. You see, the Russians will be guarding it," he said as if to a simpleton. "Guarding it heavily, I should think. Especially after they shot their main scientist for trying to escape with the plans."

"Look, if no weapons system is perfect, no security system is either, believe me. Somewhere there's a weak point and that's just where we make the snatch."

"Not we, my friend."

"You're already in Lebanon. Syria's only a few hours up the road."

"The airport, as you pointed out, is even closer."

118

"Let me put it to you this way: Do you want to be a part of Israel's destruction or Israel's salvation?"

"Oh, not again," he groaned, with his head in his hands.

"I ask you again. Are you willing to go to Syria with me to steal a laser—for Israel?"

"And for science," Jacob added. Thinking about it, he said, "This is crazy. I'm crazy. Okay. Yes. I'll go with you. But I must warn you, my soldiering skills have always lacked a certain luster."

"I don't need your soldiering skills. I need your scientific ability."

"That you've got."

"All right then, let's escort Susan to the American embassy."

"Not on your life," she said. "I'm going with you."

"No," we both said at the same time.

"Don't be stupid," I said to her. "You don't even know Arabic."

"Marhaba," she said to me.

"Okay, so after you say hello, then what?"

"Well, what do the Flying Triangles do?" she said sweetly to me.

"Talk to her, Jacob. She's your wife."

"Susan," he began.

"Shut up, Jacob."

"Susan," I said to her gently, "are you ready to be responsible for the deaths of two people who really care for you?"

"Who better to bring about your destruction than someone you love?" she said—just as gently, I might add.

"Susan, may I remind you that we have two children at home who need you?" Jacob said.

"They need you too, I might remind you. But that didn't stop you from taking off with Miriam. Well, I'm just as good as she is." She looked at him defiantly and he was silenced. "Now," she said, "what do we do first?"

There wasn't time to argue, so I gave up. "I'm not protecting

119

you, Susan. Jacob I need. But you are very expendable, so you'll have to keep up on your own."

"Right."

"She's not expendable to me," Jacob said.

At least we knew where we all stood.

"First," I said, "we get Susan some new clothes. Then we steal a pickup truck."

"Okay, let's get going!" Susan said with an enthusiasm that was totally out of place, as Jacob and I fought over who should pay for the coffee.

Chapter 18

SUSAN ENJOYED her part of the action. We went to a small boutique and she picked up a pair of jeans selling for an exorbitant price and a khaki work shirt. It could pass loosely for rough Palestinian paramilitary garb and she could slip it on after we left Beirut.

Finished with our shopping, we made our way by bus to the southern outskirts of the city. After passing by an open marketplace, I signaled to Jacob and Susan. We got off at the next stop and walked back.

As I had suspected, there were a lot of pickup trucks near the market, but most were parked in such a way that there was no possibility of making a quick departure. The most likely candidate was a green and white deal, but that would have to be backed up a hill past a row of parked cars on either side. One mistake and we'd end up either with our throats slit or in jail, neither of which had any immediate appeal.

Jacob and Susan walked with me around the marketplace. While looking for an opportunity, I was buying whatever food supplies we might need. I also picked up a few knives, ostensibly for the fruit and cheese, actually as a last resort.

Luck was with us. It was still early in the melon season and the watermelon man had sold all his crop on hand. It looked very much like he was going to pull out, back to his farm.

"Get ready, Susan. When you see which way that truck is going, run far enough in front of it to hitch a ride."

"Oh. Are you sure he'll pick me up?"

"Show some leg and smile brightly."

"Intellectually I don't approve of this."

Just then the truck seemed to turn toward the southern road. While the driver was still maneuvering his way out of the marketplace, Susan trotted her ass down the road a bit, away from the market, walking backward slowly. Jacob and I inched our way behind the truck.

Susan did a marvelous if obvious job. Hoisting her skirt up, she stuck out her thumb at the driver of the pickup. He had a man's reaction. He stopped for her. She took enough time getting into the cab of the truck to allow Jacob and me to slip in the back.

We rode roughly down the road for I guess about five kilometers. Should I have prompted Susan for the second half of this little charade or was she smart enough to figure it out on her own?

The truck pulled off the road. She was smart enough. I heard her giggling as she opened the right cab door. The driver was calling to her in Arabic to come back. She merely stood on the side of the road, smiling and indicating that she was about to unbutton her blouse. The driver came roaring out. And I came roaring down on top of him.

I socked him quickly on the side of his head, yelled at Susan to get back in the truck, yelled at Jacob to throw me some twine from the back of the truck, then tied up our friendly driver, gagging him with his own handkerchief, and rolled him into the roadside drainage ditch.

Indicating to Jacob that he should join Susan in the cab, I

climbed into the driver's seat and we were off.

"Syria, here we come," Susan shouted, enjoying herself immensely.

"Not yet," I cautioned her. "First we have to get new plates for the truck, then we've got to pick up some guns."

"How are you planning to do that?" Jacob asked.

"I don't know," I admitted.

Actually I had a good idea what I was going to do about the license plates. I circled my way north along the highway at the edge of Beirut, then cut in to the northern fringes of the city. I drove slowly through the narrow city streets until I found a truck of similar make and model to the one we were driving. I parked a few cars behind it, giving us enough room to pull out in a hurry if necessary.

"Look in the glove compartment, Jacob. Is there a screwdriver?"

Jacob fumbled with the glove compartment for a minute before he came up with one.

"Okay. Use it to remove our license plate and take it to that truck in front of us. Get his license plate and replace it with ours."

"Right," Jacob said, getting out of the truck.

"Don't you think this is rather dangerous during broad daylight with all these people around? They probably all know each other," Susan said.

"I know. We have to take that chance. The owner of this truck is going to report it stolen. I don't want to be identified because of a license plate."

"Can't you just take ours off and throw it away?"

"If you'll notice, Susan, most every car I can see has a license plate. It's little things like that you can get tripped up on."

Jacob was fast with a screwdriver, already being on the second truck. Some people stopped and watched for a few seconds. But he looked harmless and he looked as if he knew what he was doing and was doing it in a very straightforward manner. People were interested, but they were not suspicious. He was back on our truck now. We were almost home. He got into the cab. He was sweating and his hands were shaking as he put the screwdriver away. He gave me a grim grin and we were off.

We left the city of Beirut behind us and headed for Tripoli, an hour's ride, two hours at the most. The ride was pleasant. The sea was to our left as the road terraced itself along the hills.

"It reminds me of Israel," Susan said. "So stark, so beautiful."

"So dangerous," Jacob added.

We drove in relative peace until we reached the outskirts of Batroun. There we spotted two Lebanese soldiers, probably hitching a ride into the city to their homes. They were carrying guns.

"Here we go," I said to Jacob and Susan as I pulled up in front of the soldiers. "Just smile and do as I say," I said to Susan as she and Jacob followed me out of the cab.

I walked over to the two soldiers, really no more than teen-age boys, and began talking to them in Arabic. Jacob understood and though he was not too pleased, he managed to smile and say, "Good, very good piece."

I indicated to Susan that she should smile and show her merchandise. She smiled in a not very believable fashion and did a slow pivot. She swung her body from one side to the other, giving them a profile of her breasts, then she raised her skirts higher up on her hips.

"Yes, yes," they said, smiling. "How much?"

"For both of you, the same," I said. "We've had a slow day."

They both forked over a small pittance, much less than she was actually worth. Then the larger one asked where.

"In the truck," I said.

He handed his rifle to his companion and climbed into the truck. Jacob gave Susan a hefty push upward and she landed on the young soldier. I heard him giggling with delight.

We gave him a few moments with her while Jacob and I stationed ourselves behind the soldier with the guns. He smiled at us, expectantly waiting his turn. I smiled back. His attention returned to the truck. I grabbed him around the neck and gave him a short kidney punch. Jacob grabbed the guns while the soldier fell to the ground. I took one of the guns and hopped up onto the truck, pulling the soldier off Susan. He was luckily still in the midst of fondling her body. He landed on his back in the sand.

"Both of you, march!" I shouted to the soldiers. "Into the woods."

"Don't shoot. Don't shoot," they begged.

"Bring some rope," I said to Jacob, again in Arabic.

We took them into the woods while Susan waited inside the cab.

When we were far enough, I said to them, "Okay, take off all your clothes."

"All?"

"All. Get going!"

They got going. The one who had been in the truck with Susan had a head start. Then Jacob and I tied them to separate trees and started to leave.

"Why are you doing this?" one of them shouted.

"For Palestine," I answered, more or less truthfully.

We returned to the truck with the guns which we would use and the clothes which we might use. Getting back into the cab, we took off.

"Don't ever do that again, David," Susan said.

"Not ever," Jacob added.

"Should I have offered Jacob?"

"You could have just run them down," Susan said.

"Make love, not war," I countered.

"Well, you're just lucky he was young and good-looking. Otherwise I would not even have put up the pretense."

"Just remember, this wasn't my idea. You could have been safely inside the embassy by now, maybe even back in Europe."

Jointly we made our ill-tempered way past Tripoli. A few

kilometers later we pulled off the main road into the hills, threading a route through the rocks to some deserted spot where the truck couldn't be easily spotted. It was there that we would spend the night, waiting till around three the next morning, when we would drive the few short kilometers into Syria. We ate a silent, peaceful meal under the stars, drank some orange soda, the only liquid we had, then each curled into his separate sleeping place, bedding down for the night.

To: Haim Zion, Minister of Defense
From: Miriam Halevi, Paris
Subject: Jacob Sasson

I'm worried. It's past midnight and J.S. hasn't shown up on any plane arriving from Beirut. Perhaps he landed in Rome. Could you check it out?

To: Dan Tov, Chief, Section 6–3
From: Haim Zion, Minister of Defense
Subject: Beirut Fiasco

I see that no one has heard from David, the girl, or her husband for the past eighteen hours. Sleep well tonight.

Chapter 19

WAKING AT TWO-THIRTY, I lay watching the stars as the earth revolved further toward the dawn. I shattered my own serene thoughts by turning to the problems of the day, the first one being how to cross the Syrian border.

On foot of course it would have been easy to just slip across. But we needed the pickup. If there had been time to plan this operation, I would have been given the necessary maps showing the smugglers' routes, the easy paths to slip into Syria, and I would have been given Syrian identity papers. As it was, I was stuck with my own ingenuity, which unfortunately came up with nothing.

Nothing except that I needed to take a leak. I got up from my cozy little rock bed and took a look at Jacob and Susan. They were lying quite near to each other, both sleeping within the embrace of the Lebanese countryside. I made my way as quietly as possible to a more secluded spot, where I wouldn't wake them. My being away for these few moments saved us all.

When I came back, gritty, grimy, but relieved, I saw a figure standing above Susan and Jacob, a figure carrying a rifle, the rifle pointed at my married companions. Whether he was going to shoot them or wake them, I never knew. I took one of my flying leaps—no way to sneak quietly among the rocks—landed on him and brought him down, his gun crashing on the stones next to Susan's head. They were up in a matter of seconds, Jacob rushing to grab the rifle while I sat on the intruder, pinning him down.

"Who are you?" I said to him in Arabic, quite reasonably if roughly.

He spat in my face. If it's two things I really can't stand, it's spit and snot. I slapped him hard across the face several times. He started bleeding from his nose and his mouth. Blood I didn't mind. I pulled him up by the collar and thrust him back down again, his head clapping against the dirt. I raised my hand once more when he called for me to stop.

"I am Ismail, son of Yussef."

"And what do you want with us?" I snarled, pulling back my fist, making ready.

"The truck," he sputtered. "The truck would be nice to have. I thought the man and woman were campers. I was just going to tie them up and take the truck, borrow it for a short time."

"Check the truck," I said to Jacob.

He gave Susan the rifle—not a smart move, in my opinion—went over to the truck, and was back in a few minutes, carrying a bag the size of a mail sack.

Jacob opened it and spilled its contents out on the ground. Even in the moonlight the jewels glimmered from their resting place. We had with us not only a thief but hopefully a smuggler, one who would know his way across the border.

"They are precious," he said to me. "Half for you. Half."

"And why not all?" I asked. He had no answer. "What did you want with our truck anyway?" I said, getting off him and helping him up, now that Jacob had the rifle once more.

"A present for my father," he explained. "He is old now and

full of honor. The truck would signify his great status in our small village."

"And where does this honorable producer of thieves live?" He winced at the insult but answered nevertheless. "Not many kilometers hence," he said, indicating with his hand the direction toward Syria.

"A few kilometers hence. That is Syria."

"Yes. That is where I live," Ismail said, taking me for a fool, always an unfortunate mistake in dealing with me. I ran my hands along his body and through his pockets, then stood facing him. "How would you get to Syria with the truck and the jewels? You have no papers."

Ismail was not stupid in certain matters. He caught on immediately. "Ah," he said understandingly. "I will take you across the border. For a price."

"We will pay it."

"In dollars?"

"In jewels," I said, picking up his sack and holding it close to me.

Ismail was distressed. He looked at the sack, at me, then turned to look at Jacob, holding the rifle at his back.

"A good price," Ismail agreed. The deal was made.

We picked up our belongings and any evidence that we might have camped here and threw everything into the truck. Then we helped Susan into the back of the truck while Jacob and I surrounded Ismail in the cab. I started the motor and backed the pickup out onto the highway, deserted at this hour.

"Head towards Homs," Ismail instructed.

I stopped the pickup and turned off the motor. "I do not want to go across the mountains. I want to stay along the coast."

"And you will. But the route I know is fifteen kilometers up the road toward Homs. From there you catch a path that will lead you to the coastal road."

I had no choice but to believe him. We drove toward Homs and into the mountains.

"Slow," he instructed after we had passed a way on the road. "Do you see there that olive tree? Go to the right of it."

"But there is nowhere to go. This truck is not a mountain goat. It can't cross rocks like one."

"The rocks only hide a pass," Ismail explained. "Trust me."

Not likely, but I crossed the road and drove to the right of the olive tree. The truck squeezed through the rocks and we began to climb up the side of a hill, the pickup shaking as we passed over the rocks. But Ismail was right. There was a path and soon we were heading down the hill, into Syria.

The riverbed marked the dividing line between the countries of Syria and Lebanon. It was not yet dry from the summer's heat and we forded across in a primitive fashion—we got wet. But we were in Syria and soon we connected with a small dirt road taking us past the villages Ismail had promised.

"This is Kala Kadiadh. This is my home," he said. "Now just follow this road past two more villages, Haut and Tel Bibe. You will reach the coastal road before the crossing over Nahr el Haswan."

I thanked him and continued to drive.

"You have passed my home," he said to me.

"Did I?"

"Yes," he snapped.

"And in this home, do you have many brothers, many cousins?"

"Of course."

"Then you see my motives."

"We had a deal."

"The jewels for the route across the border," I said. "And you will get them. But not today."

He seethed in silence as we drove past the sleeping villages. When the main coastal road was in sight, I stopped to let him off and Susan climbed into the front seat with us again.

"Listen to me, Ismail. We have your jewels. They will buy your silence."

"What do you mean?"

"If you talk to the authorities about us, they will pick us up and you will never see this again," I said, jangling the sack before him. "But if we live, your jewels will be returned to you. We will leave them at the riverbed back there when we return to our country."

I waited for no reply, leaving him and his anger in our dust. His silence for the moment was assured. I was hoping that by the time he was ready to sell us out, we would be returning to Lebanon.

To: Haim Zion, Minister of Defense
From: Rafi Golum, Chief of Staff
Subject: Operation Bloody September

Call-up will begin at 6 a.m. tomorrow morning. The air force has been put on alert. Tanks and artillery are being moved into position. Intelligence reports indicate we shall catch them if not napping, at least nodding off.

Chapter 20

WE ARRIVED IN LATAKIA, Syria, along with the farmers heading for the marketplace. However, we did not stop at the markets, but instead made our way to the docks. Parking the truck in one of the narrow streets a few blocks away from the sea, Jacob and I changed our shirts to those of the Lebanese soldiers, ripping off all identification. With our day's growth we would look like ordinary workingmen on the make, prowling the docks.

Susan was more of a problem. She also had on her khaki shirt and jeans, but she didn't look like any workingman. Her skin was much too soft, her cheeks much too red. She didn't even look Mediterranean. Still, this was Syria's major port. Ships from all countries docked here and Western women were not unknown.

Pushing our extra clothing, the jewels and our guns under the seat, we got out and stretched our legs. I didn't know about Jacob and Susan, but I was still shaky from the ride up. We walked over to the docks and took a good look around.

French, British, Greek, Latin American—all these flags identified ships in port. Farther out at sea we saw a familiar ensign, red with hammer and sickle. The Russian cargo ships had come and were waiting for a tow to their berths.

"Okay," I said, "let's get something to eat and some rest."

We went to a small café and had breakfast—bread, salad, eggs, and most important, coffee. Then we walked the streets again, looking for an appropriate place to locate our Syrian headquarters. We found a hotel that definitely deserved the epithet seedy.

"You speak French?" I asked Jacob.

"Of course," he answered.

"Okay, we're French."

"I don't speak French," Susan pointed out.

"I didn't expect you to. But you do understand and speak a little, a few words, I hope."

"College. Two years."

"How typically American of you. Let's go."

All three of us walked in. We stood side by side in front of the desk. The clerk, a heavy old man, put down his newspaper and stood up.

"Yes, what do you want?" he asked in Arabic, assuming only too correctly that we would understand him.

"Room," I said in French, pointing up the stairs. "Room," again to make him understand.

He looked at the three of us, especially at Susan.

"Room—ghorfa," I tried hesitantly in Arabic.

He nodded yes, that he understood.

I got out some French money and handed him what I thought was appropriate.

He took the money, put it in his pocket, put out his hand again. I gave him an annoyed look and gestured with my hands. He pointed to Susan and wagged his finger no. I took out my money again and gave him more. He handed me the key to a room.

Together we climbed three flights of stairs until we found the correct number. I opened the door—a single bed, a dirty washbasin and a dirty glass. The room had one advantage. It overlooked the docks.

I went to find the bathroom. It was one floor down. I told Susan, who was not overjoyed. Matter of fact, she was not overjoyed about the whole arrangement.

"She's used to the Holiday Inn," Jacob explained.

"Well, watch the bed," I told her. "It's probably full of bugs."

She looked slightly nauseated and went over to the window to gaze out. Jacob and I sat on the bed to discuss the situation.

"We have to take turns watching the docks," I explained. "Let me go first. Then I can warn you about anything that might give you trouble."

"Okay."

"Try to get some sleep, even though in my opinion they aren't going to move their equipment out of here before tonight. I'll be back in about four hours."

"Right."

"Susan," I said to her. "Get some sleep."

"Where?" she asked as she turned up her nose at the bed.

Transmission: Call-up on Kol Israel, Gal Aleph, Bet and Gallai Zahal

David and Batsheba
Abraham's Sacrifice
Rose of Sharon
Aaron's Calf
Writing on the Wall
Ezra's Return
Daniel and the Lions
Rachel, Rachel
Behold Zion
Milk and Honey
Jonathan and David
Shlomo the Wise
Joseph and His Brothers
Exodus
The Maccabees

Chapter 21

MY TURN AT THE DOCKS was uneventful. I hung around, moving back and forth, while ships were loaded and unloaded. The Russian ships had been brought to their berths, but that was one place along the docks where there was no activity. The whole area was sealed off, patrolled by Syrian and Russian soldiers.

When it got to be around noon, I made my way slowly back to the hotel, stopping at a market stall, picking up some bread, cheese and fruit.

"It's your turn," I told Jacob, back at the hotel. "I don't think there's too much to worry about. There's a lot of activity so you can blend in. But stay away from the Russian sector. It's blocked off and the guards are keeping a close eye on everyone who passes nearby."

"Okay," he said, leaving Susan and me alone in this less than romantic situation.

I sat on the bed having lunch while Susan ate her share still staring out the window.

"Did you get any sleep?" I asked her.

"No."

"Did you get anything else?"

"None of your business!" she huffed.

"Is that all I meant to you, that you can't even give me a civil answer? I just wanted to know how everything's going between you and Jacob?"

"It's all right. He asked about you, but I diverted his attention by talking about the children."

"Hmm." I stretched in a yawn. "Why don't you come over here and lie down? You're going to need the rest."

"I'll tell you what I told Jacob—I'm not making love on any buggy bed."

"I meant to rest, honestly. You'll need it. Come on. You can lie down on me. That way the bugs won't get to you."

"Are you sure?"

"Positive."

She came over and slipped into bed, resting her body on mine. I moved my arms around her, holding her to me. Then I slowly moved my left hand down her thigh.

"Stop it," she said.

"Don't you want to tell your friends you made love in Syria?"

"Oh, yes. I can just hear Jacob asking with whom."

"It would help me a great deal," I said. "I'm very tense."

"Tense? You? I can't believe it."

"I am human, you know."

"You don't say. But I thought you were so superior."

"Well, of course I'm superior too. But I'm getting very discouraged about this whole operation. I don't see how we're going to get the laser. The dock is completely blocked off."

"Are you thinking of turning around and going back without one?"

"Yes," I admitted.

"Don't let Jacob hear you say that."

"Why not?"

"He's developed a passion for that laser device."

"That's fine. But the problem still remains: how to get it and how to get it out of here."

"You'll manage somehow. I'm sure of it."

"Thanks for the vote of confidence, Susan. But in this case your blind faith is unsettling."

"Oh, it's not blind faith," she assured me. "At this point I just don't have any alternative but to believe in you."

"Oh," I said, discouraged once more.

The hot Syrian afternoon sun began to soak through our window. We both became drowsy and at last I fell off to sleep, waking at about four, when I decided it was about time to go down and join Jacob.

"They're unloading," he said to me as we casually joined him.

Crates of various sizes were being stacked up along the docks in front of the Russian ships. If only they had workmen doing the task perhaps we could apply for the job. But again we were thwarted. Russian seamen together with the Russian army were taking care of the unloading themselves. The guards were still strung out along the dock, protecting the Russian area from any intrusion.

"Which are the lasers?" I asked Jacob.

"I would imagine it's that group of crates there, the ones with all the guards."

Another promising note.

"Look over there," Susan said.

Along the streets near the blocked-off section of the dock stood a whole parade of Russian vehicles, waiting to be loaded.

"What'll we do now?" Jacob asked.

"Get something to eat."

"Shouldn't someone watch the docks?" Susan asked.

"They're not going anyplace until dark. By that time let's hope we can come up with a plan."

We picked a little French café near the docks, Le Poisson. It was crowded already with sailors finished with their day's work and wanting a little relaxation. Most of the men inside seemed to be French seamen, but one corner of the restaurant was taken up by men in uniform, the Russian army uniform. They sat at their own little tables, just as blocked off from the rest of us by their foreignness as they were blocked off by the guards in the port. But seeing them there did give me an idea. I sat there wondering how Jacob and I would look in Russian uniforms. A little swarthy perhaps, but acceptable if it was dark enough.

"Jacob," I asked him in a low voice, "how heavy are these laser devices?"

"Oh . . ." He considered. "You'd need about four men to carry them."

"Four men!" I was outraged. "Why the hell didn't you tell me that back in Beirut?"

"You never asked me. Why? What's the problem?"

"Have you ever asked yourself how we're going to get to the laser?"

"Not really. I assumed since this venture was your idea that you had a plan."

"Well, then, this is going to come as an unpleasant surprise. I don't have a plan."

"Oh."

I watched in despair as the Russian soldiers got up en masse and left the restaurant. I had figured that stealing their uniforms would be our last chance and now they were gone.

"Russian pigs," the waiter hissed after them. They obviously had not left much of a tip, if any.

"They always come here," a French merchant officer said to no one in particular. "Every time there is a new shipment of arms, the Russians close off a section of the port, ruining our schedules, eating in our restaurants, then closing down some of the goddamn streets leading through the city. You can't take one step in Latakia without being trampled upon by some Russian."

"Yeah," I said, turning to him. "The Russians are pigs."

"Pigs," he agreed, looking hard at me. "You're Algerian, aren't you?" he asked.

"Sure, I'm Algerian," I said to him. "So what does it matter? We both speak French. I too try to make a living from the sea."

"Ah, yes," he said. "I've had some Algerian boys on my ships. Not bad. Need a talking to every once in a while."

"Me," I said, "I sail for myself. And I like to get around without any trouble. You know what I mean?"

"Smuggling, heh?"

"Let's just say I like to get around without any trouble. You said something about roads being blocked off?"

"Smuggling," he reflected. "We all have to make a living. And sailors' wages are not the best."

"No. I can imagine. Everything in life needs a little sweetener," I said, putting my hand in my pocket.

"I think I'll step outside for a breath of fresh sea air," he pronounced.

I followed him out the back way into an alley. We walked along the alley till we came to the docks once more. He brought me to where I could see the Russian convoy.

"See the trucks lined up?" he asked.

"Yes."

"Well, watch. They go down along the docks and swing in an arc up Tariq al Bab, this road here. You can see now they're starting to close Tariq al Bab and clear it of cars."

"Yes."

"Okay. So they go up Tariq al Bab one, two, three, four blocks, to a narrow road that's little more than an alley, called Shara al Madhiq. They drive straight along Shara al Madhiq until they hit the main highway out of Latakia toward Babenna."

"Across the mountains?"

"Right. If you're not going that way, you should be okay."

"Thanks. I appreciate this," I said.

140

He held out his hand. I deposited two hundred francs. He gave a small salute and was gone. I walked quickly back to the restaurant, where Jacob and Susan were gorging themselves.

"Eat up," I said, taking my place and reaching for my fork. "We've got a lot of work to do."

Susan was a slow eater, slow and neat. You could tell she had never had to scramble for her meals. We waited as patiently for her as possible. Then we were off. We walked down along the alley again to the docks and saw the Syrian soldiers still clearing the road the Russian army would use.

"Somehow," I said, "we have to find a road that's parallel to this one."

"None of these roads look very parallel," Susan said.

And how right she was. Still, we tried the road one block farther down. It was a narrow one that curved around, and we could see it was not going to take us in the direction we wanted. As we were turning back to the docks, Jacob pulled at my arm.

"An alley," he pointed out.

It wasn't even that. It was more like a sewage ditch, a gutter leading eventually to the sea. But we took it because it was going straight up.

"This reminds me of Nazareth," Susan said.

"Only smellier."

"Just don't slip," Jacob put in.

Ahead we could see that the sewage ditch crossed a narrow alley, which looked massive compared to what we had just been through. The alley was dark. There was no traffic in it.

"Stay here," I said to Jacob and Susan. Then I walked quietly along the side of the alley till I got to the end. From there I could see Syrian soldiers blocking the road perpendicular to it. I had been walking along Shara al Madhiq.

I checked the corner where the trucks were to swing into Shara al Madhiq. It was a sharp turn, which had to be negotiated carefully and, more important, slowly if the trucks were going to make it safely. And with their valuable cargo, I knew the drivers would be very, very careful.

Returning to where Susan and Jacob waited, I motioned for them to follow me. We walked along Shara al Madhiq in the other direction until we came to another road that met it, leading again to the sea. We followed this road as it curved downward and then straightened out, connecting itself to the sea road leading out of Latakia south toward Lebanon.

"This is it," I said.

"This is what?" they asked.

"The plan."

"I knew you could do it, David," Susan cheered me on.

I hadn't been so sure, but now my confidence was returning. The old mind hadn't gone yet.

"Now listen carefully. Susan, you are to take the pickup truck and drive it out of Latakia exactly fifty kilometers from this point here where these two roads converge."

"Alone?"

"Of course alone."

"But don't you remember? I don't speak Arabic."

"At this hour of the night no one is going to stop you. Just drive fifty kilometers. When you reach that point on your odometer, pull off the road to either side, left or right, depending on which looks safer. Leave the truck and place yourself someplace secure. Then if anyone comes looking at the truck, they won't find you."

"Wait for what?"

"For us. We will be heading down the highway in a Red Army truck. We'll be watching the mileage and hopefully end up at the same place as you."

"What if fifty kilometers distance is the middle of a town?"

"If it is, then go one kilometer by one kilometer until you find a safe place. If by any chance we don't meet you at the rendezvous spot by three o'clock tonight, you drive as fast as you can out of Syria. Cross the border the same way we did coming up."

"I'll never find it."

142

"You'll have to. Drive to Beirut and find the American embassy. Go back to my original idea for your getting out of Lebanon."

"Contact the CIA?"

"Right. Now remember, don't wait for us. Three o'clock. That's the limit."

"But—"

"No buts."

"Should I tell the CIA what happened?"

"Yes. And tell them to contact Mossad."

"Will they be able to help you?"

"No, but at least they'll know."

"What are you two going to do?"

"Yes," Jacob asked. "What are we going to do?"

"We are going to hijack a Russian truck. Remember that narrow road, Shara al Madhiq? You and I are going to wait at the corner there where it meets Tariq al Bab. Then we're going to jump the truck with the laser, take off down this road that we followed and catch up with Susan."

"I have some questions."

"I know, but first let's see Susan off."

We walked back to our stolen pickup and helped Susan into the driver's seat. Then Jacob and I removed our guns.

"Okay, you know where to start counting?"

"Yes."

"You'd better get going."

"You'll take care of Jacob, won't you?" she asked me.

"Yes."

"No one needs to take care of me," he said indignantly.

"Kiss me goodbye," she said.

They had an impassioned if unromantic kiss of separation before Susan took off in the pickup down the road toward Lebanon.

Chapter 22

AS WE WAVED Susan goodbye, with rifles in our hands, I decided the first thing we had to do was get rid of the guns. We scurried as casually as possible up the dark streets of Latakia, back to our own smelly little sewage ditch. But where to leave them? The ditch offered no opportunities.

We moved up to Shara al Madhiq. It remained as dark as before, though way down at its juncture with Tariq al Bab we could see the Syrians setting up lights to illuminate the corner where the trucks would need so much maneuvering.

Walking along the side of Shara al Madhiq, we thought we were nearly out of luck for a hiding place until Jacob spotted the minaret of a small mosque on the other side. We crossed the street quickly. The mosque's main entrance seemed to be on Tariq al Bab, but a small door for the impatient faithful had been provided on Shara al Madhiq. I tested it. It barely budged. Obviously not too many impatient faithful.

"We've got to get this open," I pointed out to Jacob.

Together we strained silently against the door until it began to give. Unfortunately it also began to scrape heavily on the stone walk within. But we had opened it about a foot and that was enough to place the guns inside, if only in a haphazard fashion along the edge of the inside wall. Then we pulled the massive wooden door shut.

"Are they safe?" Jacob asked.

"We'll soon know," I said.

"What do we do if they're not there when we come back?"

"Use brute force."

"I've never been very brute. I've always used my mind instead."

"Admirable," I commended him, "but in this situation you'll have to be a bit more flexible."

"What kind of brute force were you contemplating?"

"Here's the way I figure it. Now we go down to the docks and watch the trucks being loaded and leaving along the convoy route. When we see them loading the laser guidance system, we run back up here, grab the guns, and take over one of the trucks with the laser. How many lasers do you figure there are?"

"I counted at least eighty, maybe up to one hundred. They're setting up laser guidance devices for each missile system they install, so they'll need about one hundred at least to counter Israel's four hundred planes. You saw all the missiles down there. Well, they need one laser for every six to twelve missiles, depending on the coding."

"Hmm. How many lasers do you think they'll put on a truck, then?"

"I don't think they'll take any chances with the devices. I think they'll load one per truck, packed safely. But how are you planning to take the truck?"

"First we've got to see how many men are riding in each truck."

"You mean if they have guards on the truck?"

"No. I don't think they will," I said. "If it's a convoy, they'll probably have jeeps spaced out between the trucks in case of trouble. I meant how many men in the cab. If they have one man in the cab, I'll be waiting on the right side of the road, ready to jump into the driver's seat. You'll be on the left side, ready to jump into the back of the truck to protect the rear.

"If there are two in the cab, you'll have to make the jump into the back of the truck first and when you see me coming for the cab, you knock out the back window and get ready to blast if they give any trouble."

"What if the back window doesn't break?"

"You're really not too hot on this, are you?"

"I warned you I wasn't a very good soldier."

"I know and I understand. But we're so close to it now, I don't want to let it go by, especially since we no longer have a truck of our own to escape with."

"Right. But how do you plan to take the truck? Won't it be going too fast? Won't the trucks in front and behind notice something wrong?"

"Not if we act efficiently. You see, where Tariq al Bab meets Shara al Madhiq, that's a tight corner. That's why the lights are being strung, so the Russians won't run into the wall. This means that the trucks are going to be going slow, very slow. Now, we have to get to that truck with the laser device just after it turns the corner and straightens out and before another truck takes the corner. The driver will be in shock for the first few moments; chances are that he'll follow instructions, move over and give me the wheel. You'll keep your gun pointed at the window. I'll inform him of that. No one wants to die, even for Mother Russia. Then I turn off the lights, drive down that side street we located and onto the main highway out of Latakia, the same way Susan went."

"Okay, but by that time the next truck will have turned into Shara al Madhiq."

"Yes, but if we're lucky the driver won't notice us because he'll be busy maneuvering. And even if someone notices us, what can he do? The truck in front may notice a blank spot in its rear-view mirror. The truck behind might notice something

146

wrong. But is it going to take after us when its responsibility is to deliver its merchandise safely? Its only alternative is to honk and no security jeep can follow us since the trucks are blocking the way. Don't worry. It will work."

Jacob was not calmed by my reassurances. Still, we made our way back to the docks, finding ourselves a dark recess from which to watch the loading of the convoy. As Jacob had pointed out earlier, the guards were heavy around the laser devices, and the lasers were not the first to be loaded. Obviously the attempted defection of the scientist had left the Russians uneasy.

We watched the slow, heavy process as the fork lifts carried the cargo from the docks and onto the trucks, the trucks then moving off slowly on their route out of the city. It was taking longer than I had planned for, and I was getting worried about the timing.

"What are they carting off now?" I asked him.

"The missiles. Finally."

I looked at my watch. Jacob saw me.

"What time?" he asked.

"One-thirty."

"I didn't realize. It's getting late."

"Not too late. We still have another hour before we have to panic. It doesn't take that long to cover fifty kilometers. And even if Susan does start out, we'll still be able to catch her."

"Hopefully," he added. "Did you really make a living doing this?"

"Yes."

"How did you stand it? I'd give everything to be back in Ann Arbor with the kids climbing all over me."

"I never had any kids. That's the difference. Anyway, I'm retired now."

"Yeah, it looks it."

"No, this is all a mistake. I got into this by helping Susan locate you."

"Well, I don't know how you can remain so cool."

"I'm not cool. I'm sweating all over, besides being scared shitless."

"Oh, yeah? That makes two of us, then."

"Three. Don't forget Susan down the road."

"Look," he said, grabbing me by the arm.

I turned my attention back to the docks. They were loading the lasers, loading them one at a time into small trucks, only a little larger than our pickup. They loaded them, covered them with a tarp, then lashed them down.

"Let's go," Jacob said.

"Not till we see how many in the cab."

"I forgot."

The lasers were being checked off. The drivers were signing a sheet of paper, locating the code on each box, noting the trucks' license numbers, and presumably recording both.

Then the drivers moved toward the trucks. Three were already packed and ready to go. Only one driver. Only one person in the cab. We were in! I gave Jacob a smile and we made our dash for Shara al Madhiq.

Chapter 23

Retrieving our guns wasn't as easy as we had planned it to be. With my lack of foresight, which was becoming endemic, I forgot that Shara al Madhiq would no longer be a dark passageway but would be ablaze with the headlights of Russian trucks. Luckily there was not a steady stream of them, just one rolling after another at lengthy, regular intervals.

I told Jacob to make his way on up to about fifteen feet from the corner of Shara al Madhiq and Tariq al Bab. I myself was going for the guns. He looked doubtful and wished me luck. I waited till one truck had passed our smelly little alley, then made a dash across the street for the door to the mosque. As I inched my way up my side of the street, I saw Jacob moving up the other side.

I came to the door and managed to push it open. Then I slid down to reach my hand inside for the guns. I didn't feel them. I couldn't believe it. No matter what I had told Jacob, right now my security was bound up in those guns and they were missing. I began to sweat profusely. I steadied myself against the door and took a few deep breaths, relaxing my muscles, or attempting to. I probed through the crack again and felt for the guns. This time I was rewarded by touching upon something cold and metallic. Our guns. They had slid from where we leaned them against the wall and had fallen flat on the stones. Relieved, I drew them slowly out through the crack and pulled the door shut. Then I stood up.

Headlights flashed upon me. A Russian driver stuck his head out of his window and shouted something in Russian. How ridiculous of him to think an Arab peasant would understand. But like Americans, Russians only speak more slowly and loudly in their own language, thinking all the time that this makes what they're saying understandable. I merely turned my back on him, unbuttoned my pants and pretended to pee. While doing that I smiled and waved at him as stupidly as possible. He grumbled something and pulled off. I rebuttoned my pants and ran like hell up Shara al Madhiq before another truck could catch me in its headlights.

Jacob was in place. I ran his gun over to him.

"Be ready to move," I whispered. "The second truck with a laser. That's the one we take. Remember, jump in the back and have your gun ready, pointed through the cab at the driver."

"Right."

We pressed our bodies against the wall as another Russian truck passed us by. The driver's attention was taken by trying to straighten out his truck so it could be moved through the narrows of Shara al Madhiq. At that moment he had no eyes for us.

I slipped back over to my side, checking my watch. Two-fifteen. Now all we needed was for a truck to have a flat tire and stop the convoy entirely. A huge carrier came by with what I hoped were the last of the missiles. Yes. We could hear the next truck. A smaller engine. It came into view. It was the first truck carrying a laser. It made its turn carefully, carefully and slowly, and then passed us by. I signaled to Jacob to get ready.

The next truck with the laser pulled up to make its turn. I saw the red star flashing on the side of its cab. The driver, a young blond boy, pulled his wheel sharply to the right. He negotiated the turn and then straightened the wheel and began driving ahead.

I ran for the cab, my gun slung across my back, and grabbed at the door handle from the inside. The boy driver looked startled. I opened the door, leaped up onto the seat and pushed him over. He hit his head on the passenger door, but had moved his body enough for me to take over the wheel and straighten out the truck, which had swerved slightly and was heading for the wall.

I barked something out at the kid in Arabic, which he obviously didn't understand. Then I nodded my head back toward the window. He looked. Jacob was there pointing his gun.

The kid was still startled, but I knew it wouldn't take him long to recover and make some grandstand play. We were nearing our turnoff. I pushed off the lights and stepped on the gas. We sped down our narrow escape route and were just about to hit the sea road out of Latakia when the Russian made his move. He tried to open the passenger door. I grabbed him by the collar and smashed his head against the dashboard. He sank into oblivion on the floor of the cab. Then I turned my attention back to driving the truck, which had careened onto the main highway, cutting off an old De Soto.

I pushed my foot down on the gas pedal and we really moved. Jacob was tapping on the window, looking worried, probably because he did not see the Russian. I gave him the okay sign and he smiled.

Now it was just a matter of finding Susan. I slowed the truck down to a respectable speed. When we turned from Shara al Madhiq, I had heard no noise, no honking, no gunfire, no nothing. I hoped that meant that we were not missed. It had been fast; it had been efficient. We might be in luck.

The kilometers ticked by, twenty, thirty, forty. We passed through Baniyas. Forty-seven, forty-eight, forty-nine, we passed the Crusader castle, Qalat el Marqab, sitting high on the hill alongside us. Fifty. I slowly pulled the truck off the road. I could see the castle in the background. I flashed my lights, then turned them off.

I got out of the cab and Jacob whispered, "Where is she?"

"I don't know." I couldn't see the truck and I should have been able to.

We heard a rock fall on the other side of the road. Then another rock was tossed in our direction.

"Susan?" I said in a normal voice.

"Is that you?" she whispered.

Jacob jumped off the truck. "Where are you?" he called.

"Jacob!" she said, rushing across the road and into his arms.

"Where's the truck?" I asked, my voice, I must admit, a little bit tinged with jealousy.

She came over and gave me a hug, saying, "I left it on the other side of the road."

"Where are the keys?"

"Here," she said, handing them to me. Then she led me over to the truck. She had driven it right into the rocks.

"Don't worry, it's safe," she assured me. "I already tried to back it out and it moved right away."

I gave her a doubtful look but she proved correct. I backed up across the road and brought our pickup tail to tail with the Russian truck. We set to work.

"Gather some sticks," I told Susan.

Meanwhile Jacob and I unlashed the case containing the laser and threw off the tarp. Jacob patted the box and gave it a big kiss. We smiled at each other. Susan returned with various sizes of wooden sticks.

"Okay. When we lift the box, shove the sticks underneath so we can roll it."

It was a slow and laborious process, some of the sticks being crunched into nonexistence, but we finally moved the laser to the tailgate. We had arranged the trucks so that our tailgate was

152

underneath the Russian one. Now would come the most difficult move, the move from one truck to the other.

"Wait," Jacob said. "Let's wrap a rope around this and you get on top of our cab and pull it while we push."

"But Susan's not that strong."

"She's strong enough to push it with the sticks still underneath. But when they roll out, we need someone at the other end making sure the damn thing doesn't crash through the tailgate. If it hits the ground, you might as well kiss it goodbye."

"Okay."

We lassoed the box and I moved up front.

"Okay—when I count three," Jacob said. "One. Two. Three!"

They pushed and I pulled. The box careened across the tailgates and landed in our pickup, just barely. Then we again went back to the laborious process of rolling it along the sticks closer to our cab so there would be no chance of its falling out.

While we were lashing the laser back into place, we heard the cab door of the Russian truck open. It was the young driver. He was making a dash for it along the sand. I jumped off the truck and followed.

He was a fast runner but he was hurt; and I managed to tackle him not too far away. I brought him back and got some of the spare rope out of the truck.

Susan started to say something, but I motioned her to keep quiet. I didn't want him to hear us speak anything but Arabic although the chances were unfortunately good that he had heard us talking while we were moving the box. But no use in impressing it upon his mind.

He was young and scared when I took him over to the other side of the road and tied him up in a tight and uncomfortable position. Then, gagging him securely, I placed him so that he would be hidden by the rocks. If he was in luck, the shepherds would find him tomorrow.

Now we had one thing left to dispose of. The Russian truck. Of course it would be exposed in the dawn but for now I drove it straight out into the sea. Then I floated out of the cab and swam back to our truck.

I said, "Jacob, stay in the back. If there's trouble, we'll have to shoot our way through. Susan, you take my gun. Do you know how to shoot?"

"No."

"Wonderful. All right, look, it's simple. I'm taking the safety off and switching it to automatic. Now it will work like a machine gun. You just pull the trigger and it will shoot out a whole splat of bullets. So be careful."

"No wonder men join the army while women stay home to cook."

"Oh, why's that?"

"This is simpler."

"I never looked at it that way before. I thought it had something to do with human sensitivity."

"Men being less sensitive?"

"Better able to hide it," I said.

"Look, let's move on out of here," Jacob said. "If you're going to discuss woman's place with Susan, we'll be here all night and it will just end up with her screaming at you."

"You're right," I said, looking at the sky. "Let's go."

Transmission 12–1
To: Nassem Nasri, Chief, Section 8–2
From: Agent H-7
Subject: Russian Arms Shipment

Unreliable report lacking early confirmation has come in on Russian movements. Report says one Russian laser guidance device is missing. Russians are now going through the process of checking it out, but it is almost impossible at this early hour as the arms are still in transit. They are using helicopters for the search.

Will keep you posted.

Copy to Haim Zion, Minister of Defense
Could it be our missing Wonder Boy?
                    Nassem

To: Amos Bakshi
From: Dan Tov
Subject: David Haham

Amos,
    I'm worried about David. Neither he nor the Sasson woman
has shown up in any of the logical places.
1. Have you heard from him?
2. Should I feel guilty about this?
3. Do you think he'll be all right?

To: Dan Tov
From: Amos Bakshi
Subject: David Haham

1. No.
2. Yes.
3. Yes.
Don't bother me again unless you hear from him. I'll be busy
the next few days.

To: Haim Zion, Minister of Defense
From: Rafi Golum, Chief of Staff
Subject: Operation Bloody September

    All personnel are in place. Air force will begin bombard-
ment at 0430. Army maneuvers will begin at 0500. Naval
action will coincide with infantry attacks.
    Code word: Remember Ma'alot.

Chapter 24

MY GREATEST FEAR now was that we would be caught along the Syrian-Lebanese border. It was already three-thirty and it would take us at least another hour to reach the border. By then the early morning light would have come to the Mediterranean. Even now the morning star was on the horizon and rising in an all too rapid fashion.

As we drove along the sea road, we began to pick up more traffic, mainly farmers getting an early start. Several shepherds were already moving their flocks to new pastures. It would all be very picturesque if you didn't have a Russian laser guidance system in the back of your truck.

We crossed the Nahr el Haswan and forked off to the dirt road taking us through the villages and to the smugglers' route out of Syria. We would keep our word and drop the jewels along the riverbed, we hoped. It was daybreak. We could be seen. We could be seen by our friendly smuggler Ismail and his honorable father, not to mention his brothers and cousins. It was blood with Ismail, this deal of ours, blood and honor and money. I held my breath as we passed through Kala Kadiadh, Ismail's village.

A few early morning fires had been started, a few movements, but no band of men waiting to tear us to pieces. We passed through the town safely. I gave Jacob the thumbs up sign out the window. Our celebration was entirely out of place.

We hit the riverbed and were ambushed. No shooting yet. But men came out of their hiding places and blocked the way of our truck. Unfortunately I had no speed with which to run them down; the truck had been inching along. I was trying to avoid as much jostling as possible with the laser in the back.

A familiar figure swaggered over to my side of the cab. "And now you see before you my family," Ismail the smuggler said, smiling.

I gave them all the greetings of Allah. I'm not averse to the amenities if they get us out of trouble.

"Did you like our scene back in the village?" he asked.

"Yes, very convincing," I flattered him. "I expected no trouble."

"I do not forget a slight."

"We made a deal," I said. "We have your jewels."

Taking that as a signal, Jacob tossed them down to Ismail. Ismail threw the sack to one of his brothers, or was it a cousin?

"But now I want more than that because, you see, now it is I who hold the gun."

"What do you want? Perhaps we can make a deal."

"I want the woman."

Luckily Susan didn't understand Arabic. She sat there calm and collected, relatively. "What do you want the woman for?"

"To sell."

"She is old."

"She is blond. She will bring money."

"You can't have her," I said, realizing that Jacob probably loved Susan more than the laser. Not that I would have actually bargained her away on my own.

"I want the truck for my father."

"Your honored father, Ismail, deserves a better truck than

this. Buy him one from your profit on the jewels."

"And I want what is in your truck."

"You have no use for what is in the truck."

"We are not bargaining," Ismail said. "You are denying everything I desire. Are you forgetting that this is my marketplace? Oh. I forgot to tell you. I also want your life. You have dishonored me. But first let us see what prize I have gotten in the back of your truck."

"Show him, Jacob!" I shouted, hoping he would catch my meaning.

As Ismail left the side of the cab, I stepped on the gas, churning my way across the riverbed while Jacob indeed showed Ismail what he had. The automatic cut down a few of Ismail's brothers and cousins, perhaps Ismail himself. I didn't stay to look. We had caught them by surprise and were speeding, if you could call it that, up the hill before they opened fire. Jacob was doing a good job of keeping them down. We were up and over the hill. Then Jacob stopped firing. I hoped it was because we were safe and not because he had been hit. I made my way down the hill at a record if unsafe speed and slipped past the olive tree out onto the main highway. I raced down toward Tripoli, afraid the shooting would bring an immediate response from the border guards.

"How's Jacob?" I asked Susan when we were safely making our way down the road with no sign of any official following.

She contorted her body to look out the rear window. "He's holding his head."

"Is he hurt!"

She looked again. "No, just aggravated."

By the time we got to Tripoli we needed gas. We pulled over into a roadside station that had a small café attached to it. After filling up, we all got out to stretch and to get something to eat.

"Where's the gun?" I asked Jacob.

"Under the tarp."

"How's the box?"

"In one piece. Two bullet holes hit the upper edge, but I don't think it hurt the merchandise. More damaging was your driving back there."

"What was I suppose to do, stay and get killed?"

I walked around to the rear of the truck and checked the tires. They would last, I thought. Then Jacob and I sat down at an outside table, keeping a close eye on the truck. Susan returned from the washroom and joined us.

"This place is never going to get four stars from Bazak, let me tell you."

We ordered breakfast, then I turned to Jacob and said, "You know, before this trip I never knew how simple Susan's needs are. All she wants is a clean, unbuggy bed and a sparkling white toilet."

"And a husband," he added.

"You two are so goddamned superior. You feel like he-men just because you got some goddamned Russian laser out of Syria and past those bandits back there. I think both of you are suffering from swagger of the mouth."

"You don't think we did a good job?" Jacob asked, proud of himself.

"What do you mean, you? While you two were holding hands in Latakia, I was hiding in the rocks alone, next to hysteria any time a car passed."

"Ahh," Jacob and I both said together.

"Wait till I get you home, Jacob. Then you'll see how smartsy you're going to be."

Breakfast came and we stuffed ourselves. The bread was warm, the first of the day, and it made up for the salad, which tasted like it had been left over from last night.

"Now what do we do?" Jacob asked.

"We drive south. Past Sidon we take the road which cuts across Lebanon toward Metulla."

"Metulla? That's Israel," Susan said.

"That's the whole idea," I pointed out to her.

"But how do we get there is what I meant. They have fences and everything."

"They also have border defense roads built for the Israeli army for patrol inside Lebanon. I know of one of those roads just west of Metulla. It's this road we'll try to hit."

"So we should be there in how long?" she asked.

"It's—let's see—five-thirty now; no, almost six. Roughly four to five hours, without any trouble. With trouble, God only knows."

"So we might be there in time for lunch."

"What sort of trouble are you expecting?" Jacob asked.

"The Palestinians. Remember I told you they were preparing for war? Well, they should be gathering along the borders of Israel now."

"We might not get there in time for lunch," Susan reconsidered.

"And we have to go through them?" Jacob asked.

"Right. There's no other way. We'll have to bluff our way through. Just leave it to me. If the bluff doesn't work, well, we have two guns and the example of Trumpledor. Let's get started."

Chapter 25

WE GOT BACK into the truck, Jacob again guarding the laser. Then we started driving south toward Beirut. We passed through a lot of little hamlets along the way, even some respectably sized towns, and everywhere we went we became aware that groups of men were clustered around the local cafés. This was not so unusual. Many men spent their whole waking hours at the local café, but these were larger groups of men, and younger, not just a few who had nothing else to do. It made me uneasy. It was our first sign that something was definitely wrong.

We passed through Beirut, using the highway along the outskirts of the city, and then returned to the coastal road, leaving the traffic from the city behind us. We made it as far as Ed Damur, where a roadblock was put up in our path. There was no way out of it. Cars in front of us, cars behind, and Lebanese soldiers guarding the road.

"Are they looking for the laser?" Susan asked.

"No, I don't think so. Why would they block the road down here looking for a laser stolen in Latakia?"

"So what's happening?"

"I don't know. Whatever it is, it's not to our benefit."

Few cars were allowed to pass through the roadblock. Most were turned around and headed back toward Beirut. To these returning cars were added more from the south, many of them loaded with suitcases and seven or eight people, whole families fleeing the area.

I flagged down one of these cars. "What's happening?" I yelled to the driver.

"The Israelis. They've invaded all of southern Lebanon."

"Where?"

"Along the southern and western borders. Turn around, turn around. They came with tanks, planes, everything."

"But the Palestinians are there."

"Yes, all the Palestinians. Our land will be fertile next year. It will be drenched in blood. Turn around now. Save yourself," he yelled as he sped off toward the safety of the north.

I thought to myself, Don't panic. Here I was in a trap of my own making. It was the third day. And I had suggested to Dan Tov that this be the day the Israeli army should invade Lebanon to destroy the Palestinians. I should be getting some kind of perverse pleasure out of my battle strategies. Instead I was suffering from sweaty palms.

"Jacob," I yelled at the back of the truck. "Come down."

Jacob jumped down, thank God without his gun, and walked alongside the truck.

"Did you hear?" I asked.

"Everything."

"We've got to get through. Otherwise we're going to rot here. After we're dead. We have to have a story. Okay? We're Palestinians, got it? We're bringing guns to our brothers in the south. If the Lebanese don't buy that story, don't shoot. There are too many soldiers with too many guns. We'll be slaughtered. We'll just turn around and try to get another road out."

162

"Right."

He hopped back into the truck as we inched farther toward the roadblock.

"What's happening?" Susan asked. I had forgotten that she couldn't understand Arabic.

"There's a war in the south. The Israelis have attacked the Palestinian encampments."

"Oh, my God! What are we going to do?"

"Go through it."

"Go through it? The war?"

"Yes."

"David, this is insane."

"I know."

"David, we're going to be killed."

"I know, I know."

"I have two children at home who love their mommy."

"I know."

"Then turn back."

"I can't."

"Turn back. There's got to be another way."

"Like what?"

"Like," she thought, "by the sea. How about that? Hiring a boat."

"We have no money, we have no papers, and no one's going to take a boat out while there's a chance of Israel's attacking by sea."

"Then go to the American embassy. Tell them what we have. I'm sure they'll welcome you with open arms."

"Where? When the students wake up and news of this war reaches them, the American embassy is the first place they'll head for. In a few hours there's not going to be an embassy to welcome us."

It was our turn. A Lebanese soldier looked into the cab and back at Jacob. "Where are you going?" he asked.

"To the front," I said bravely.

"Where to the front? Don't you know the Israelis have invaded?"

"Of course. We go to fight for our land."

"It's senseless now. They're slaughtering you down there."

"We must fight for our homeland."

"What's in the back of your truck?"

"Weapons for Palestine."

"What kind of weapons?"

"Antitank."

"You'll need them. At least let the woman stay."

"She is a freedom fighter. She is one of us."

He shrugged his shoulders and signaled his companions to lift the blockade.

"Good luck," he shouted, "God be with you." Then he tapped the truck on its side and sent us on our way, south toward Israel, south toward the war.

Chapter 26

"SO FAR SO GOOD," I said as our truck jiggled its way down toward Sidon.

"You've got to be kidding," Susan shouted at me. "You maniac! You think you're going to drive this truck safely through a war zone?"

"As we say in Israel, the improbable we do immediately, the impossible takes a little longer."

"Well, you're not in Israel, you fucking idiot. You're in Lebanon. And I'm probably going to be killed by an Israeli bullet."

"Don't get hysterical, Susan. I mean, after all, who is going to notice one little truck?"

"The planes, the tanks, the artillery, the infantry."

"Let's try to keep this thing on an upbeat," I said to her.

She buried her head in her hands and moaned, "What am I doing here?"

"*I* should ask *you* that. If you'll remember, it was because of you that we wound up in this mess."

"How was it my fault?" she screamed.

"You're the one who had to fly to Beirut to follow Jacob. And

I followed you. If you had only waited another day, he would have flown to New York."

"No one asked you to follow me."

"On the contrary."

"Well I didn't."

"Well Dan Tov did."

"Well if you're going to listen to that half-assed moron, don't put the blame on me."

"Oh shut up and keep your eyes on the road. And keep your gun ready."

"And to think just a few days ago I had romantic illusions about you."

"And I had romantic illusions about you. I had even begun to develop a taste for meaty ladies."

"Oh," she screamed, taking a swipe at me.

"Goddamn it," I screamed, lifting my hand to protect myself from her nails. The truck swerved off the road into the sand. I pulled it too sharply back onto the road. It tipped to the left and felt like it was going over.

"Lean right! Right!" I yelled.

I pushed my body toward Susan, who, either to get out of my way or from understanding, leaned on the passenger door. The truck straightened up but the passenger door flew open. Susan screamed as her body slipped out the door. I made a grab for her hair and pulled her in, the truck sliding across the road from my inattention. I slammed my foot on the brake and we came to a screeching halt. The truck shook as Jacob's body flew against the cab.

"Close the door," I said to Susan in a low, calm voice.

She closed it and locked it. I heard Jacob screaming from the rear of the truck, but I paid no attention to him. One hysterical member of this family was all I could stand at a time. I drove slowly onward, taking deep breaths and counting to one hundred.

As we were coming up on Sidon, we noticed a heavy increase

of Lebanese army traffic. I wondered if they were going to join in on this war. Several times we were waved off the road, taking a short detour through the dirt to make room for the Lebanese tanks rolling south.

Finally at Sidon we hit another roadblock. There wasn't much of a line here. All civilian vehicles were moving north. It was just us, a few other nuts, and the Lebanese army moving south. Our turn came.

"Where are you going?" a mustachioed sergeant asked.

"To Marj Uyun to join our brethren on the front lines."

"You are Palestinian?"

"Yes."

He spat into the dirt. Obviously not one of our fans.

"Is the Lebanese army coming to join us?" I asked.

"No. We make a line here. If the Israelis try to move up after they wipe you out, we will be ready."

"They won't wipe us out."

"That's not what the reports are saying."

"Have they landed by sea?"

"Several landing parties from Tyre on down. They have you in a nutcracker and are beginning to squeeze."

I shifted my legs nervously. "How about from here to Marj Uyun?"

"Groups of your brothers along the way working up their enthusiasm for paradise. Around Marj Uyun a lot of fighting. The Israelis have pushed across from Metulla."

"Well, thanks for the information."

"See you in heaven," he said, waving us on.

"What was that all about?" Susan asked as we pulled back on the road.

I gave her a sickly grin and watched the road carefully. Soon we would fork to the left, heading straight for Metulla, if we ever made it.

The road wasn't crowded. The Palestinians must have all been moved into forward positions, training for their assault on

Israel when Syria gave the signal, because so far we had not encountered any troops. A few stragglers crossed our path, a few deserters perhaps, but that was it.

After Nabatiya, when we were only twenty kilometers from the border, things changed. We noticed that immediately when a Phantom flew low over us and tried to drop a bomb in the back of our truck. I took evasive action, rolling the truck all over the road, finally pulling off the road when I saw him swoop down again. It was a lucky move on my part, as he blew the road to pieces right alongside us. Then he took off, looking for more important targets, the blue star of Israel blazing in the sun.

"Oh, this is just great!" Susan shouted.

"Shut up, will you! What do you want me to do?"

"Losing your cool, Mr. Superior? What about poor Jacob out there in the open?"

I quickly turned my head around and caught a glimpse of Jacob crouched in the corner, looking kind of sick.

Meanwhile a formation of three Phantoms came from the southern skies, made a turn to the left of us and streaked off to the west, probably supporting the invasions by sea.

We were making slow progress. The pickup rattled in the dust. Several times I attempted to get back on the road, each time finding that the road only existed in small stretches between bomb craters.

Now we could hear the artillery loud and clear, the boom boom of the pieces as each side tried to splatter the other to death. We were no longer the only traffic in the area. On the other side, across from us, small trucks like ours were carrying piles of wounded men, hoping to make it back to Sidon and relative safety. These were the lucky ones.

But our luck had again run out. Ahead I could see what looked like divisional headquarters for the area. Soldiers were scurrying all over, boxes of ammunition lay stacked next to unused rifles and artillery pieces. To one side was a Red Cross tent trying to take care of the wounded being brought back from the front. Scattered among all this were several small fires, buildings shattered, men dying. The Phantoms had come but had not finished the job.

We were waved to the side. I drove on for a while, trying to pick my way through the rubble, looking for a way out of the encampment. But soldiers came running after us.

"Halt! Halt!" they shouted, rifles ready.

"Okay, okay," I said.

A man about my age came up to the window on Susan's side. I assumed that he was in a position of authority, as he had survived to a ripe old age for a terrorist.

"Where are you going?" he asked.

"To the front."

"No, you're not going anywhere. No trucks further up."

"I have my orders. They come from Mohammed Sadeq. I'm to take these weapons to the front."

"All weapons remain here. This is the front for you. Now pull the truck over and get out."

"I have my orders."

"You have your orders from me," he said, pulling out his pistol.

I shot the truck into first and pulled away from him.

"Your gun!" I shouted to Susan. "Use your gun!"

I don't think she even realized she was being fired at, because without ducking, she stuck her gun out the window and pulled the trigger. It automatically spat out the bullets.

"They're falling! They're falling! Do you think I shot them? Oh, my God, no!"

"Don't worry, they probably just tripped," I said, trying to stave off her woman's conscience.

Meanwhile I could hear Jacob firing from the rear. Only he was being more selective. A flash of orange scorched across my rear-view mirror. Jacob had fired into the ammunition.

We sped out of the camp, as fast as a truck could go through the pockmarked earth. Now the sounds of the artillery were right upon us. I had a feeling we would face no more road-blocks. We would face death and either live or die. Now there was no other alternative.

Chapter 27

WE HAD REACHED the Palestinian front, or what was left of it. There were pockets of resistance. Some of the Palestinians were going to fight until they were wiped out one by one. Others were retreating in a more orderly fashion than I would have given them credit for. They would run back a way, turn and fire, then run back again. No one paid any attention to us as we passed through the Palestinian lines. They were all too busy fighting for their lives.

Then came that incredible moment when we were in between the two lines. I remember thinking that suddenly in the midst of war we had found a moment of peace. Behind us the rifles and machine guns shot past. In front of us the Israeli tanks made a steady line, an invincible line, their cannons mowing down all who dared to stand in front of them.

And there we were, standing in front of them. It took the tanks a little while to catch on to the fact that a pickup truck was coming toward them. Or perhaps it was just the time it took for the commander to plot the coordinates and shout them to the gunner.

I had hoped that maybe, just maybe, we could run through the line of tanks before they fixed on us, but I saw the cannon of the tank facing us on the left swivel toward us. I maneuvered the truck as fast as I could, pulling it to the left of the tank and trying to swing past it before its cannon got us in sight again. But the tank to the left of that one zoomed its cannon in on us and I knew we were in a cross fire.

I stomped on the brakes and slammed the truck into reverse, moving just in time to watch the cannon fire cross right over the top of our hood.

"Underneath the seat!" I shouted to Susan. "Find my white shirt and wave it!"

Susan crouched down and reached beneath the seat while I drove the truck like some crazy man, trying to avoid the tanks. I saw her head slam against the dashboard several times and only hoped she didn't pass out before she reached the shirt.

She had it. I saw a flash of white. She held onto it with her fist and waved it out the window. I turned the truck parallel to the line of tanks and drove along in front of them, making sure they all saw the white shirt and got the idea. Yes, we were surrendering. And to our allies. Then I turned the truck around and made my decision to try to drive through the lines.

The two tanks between whom I was planning to drive saw me coming. Two soldiers shot out from their respective turrets, their guns pointed straight at us, warning us that if this was a suicide mission, we would be succeeding only too well.

"We're Israelis! We're Israelis!" Jacob and I shouted at them as we passed by.

"What's the matter?" one of the soldiers shouted back. "You missed the road to Haifa?"

There were tears in my eyes as I drove farther into the Israeli lines and saw our soldiers moving up. Susan continued to wave the white shirt and they gave us curious glances, probably wondering about the Lebanese license plates among other things.

"Hey! Stop that truck!" someone shouted as we pulled slowly along.

We were immediately surrounded by bright young kids casually pointing around twenty rifles in our direction.

I stopped the truck and got out. Jacob had laid down his gun and jumped out from the back and was going around to help Susan.

I announced to the crowd at large, "I'm David Haham." The kids looked at each other and shrugged. So fleeting is fame.

One of them, a corporal headed for bigger things, shouted at a group of officers, "He says he's David Haham."

"David! David Haham!" I heard a voice call back. A burly man with goggles slung around his neck rushed over to me. It was Haim. He was a full colonel in the tank corps. We had trained together. We fell on each other like long-lost brothers, hugging and kissing, then hugging again.

"What," he finally asked, "what in God's name are you doing here?"

"Bringing one of the Russian laser guidance systems back from Syria."

"What!" he shouted in disbelief. Then he roared, "Oh, is that all. I thought you might be involved in something important."

Just then an artillery shell landed too close for comfort.

"Bastards!" Haim shouted, raising his fist. "I thought we knocked out all their artillery." He screamed at his group of officers. "Call the goddamn air force. Tell them to move their butts and knock out that piece. They expect us to do everything," he said to me.

Jacob came up to us. "Look," he said. "I don't want to interrupt a reunion, but don't you think we'd better get this laser to safety? I don't want to lose it now."

"Who's he?" Haim asked.

"Jacob Sasson. We got it out together."

"And the woman?" Haim asked again.

"My wife," Jacob answered.

"Do you think you really should have involved her in this?" Haim asked. He shook his head disapprovingly at us, and then went over to the field phone.

After speaking for a minute, he came back. "Your friend's down the road, interrogating some Palestinians we picked up."

"Who?"

"The one from Shin Bet."

"Amos Bakshi?"

"Yeah, that's his name. Don't sneak up on him, though. I think he's still in a state of shock that you should be here. You want an escort?"

"Yes!" Susan shouted.

So we got back into our truck while Haim ordered a jeep in front of us and behind. They accompanied us to, of all places, Metulla.

"Well, Susan," I said, looking up into the sky, "we're right on schedule. It's lunchtime."

To: Haim Zion, Minister of Defense
           Dan Tov, Chief, Section 6–3
From: Amos Bakshi
Subject: David Haham

The lost sheep has come home and with him Jacob and Susan Sasson. He has also brought something you might be interested in—the laser guidance system for the Russian SAM-12 missiles.

To: Haim Zion, Minister of Defense
From: Dan Tov, Chief, ·Section 6–3
Subject: Completion of Operation Syrian Hijack

Dear Haimele,
   I'm not going to say that I had this in mind all the time, but this is just another outstanding achievement you can add to my list of credits. Sorry I had to keep you in the dark on this so long.
   By the way, congratulations on the war.

                             Love,
                             Danny

Chapter 28

THE REST OF THE STORY is what you might expect. We made our way to Amos and told him what we had. He called in a transport helicopter and had the laser loaded into it. Jacob scrambled into the helicopter and held on to the laser the way a doctor would hold on to a sick patient. Susan and I made our way to the front of the copter with the pilot. We lifted off, landing later at an army base in the Negev, where the general in charge told us he had a sumptuous meal prepared. We wanted a bath first. All except for Jacob. He wouldn't leave the laser.

By evening the war was over. Only the mopping up was left to do. By the next day southern Lebanon was free of the terrorists for the first time in many years. Then Israel withdrew. Of course the terrorists would be back. Soon they would rebuild themselves and try to slip across our borders, ready to attack their usual military targets, our women and children. But it would be a long time before they considered themselves a fighting army again, except in their fantasies.

There would be no war with Syria. For some unaccountable

reason, Syria and Russia had had a slight falling out which resulted in Russia's pulling out of Syria its laser guidance system. The Russians would probably try to modify the laser system, but it didn't matter. Now we knew what they knew—how to build the system and, more important, how to counter it.

The Americans sent a scientific team from their army to join us in the Negev. They took the laser apart piece by piece, Jacob being foremost among them, until it had no more secrets to yield.

Susan sat alongside the swimming pool, bitching about how she was being neglected. I tried to pay attention to her, but she kept saying, "I couldn't, I just couldn't any more. Not that I wouldn't want to, you understand."

I understood.

Thinking I should do something for Jacob and Susan Sasson to show them the free world's appreciation for their valiant efforts, I arranged payment for them from the CIA into a Swiss bank account, reminding the CIA that it had recruited Susan for this mission. At least it would help put the Sasson kids through college.

Seven days later I was seeing them off at Lod airport. The occasion was a happy one. I had by then received my customary note of gratitude from the prime minister. They had received their Swiss bankbook. We all embraced and kissed each other goodbye. I saw them pass through the gates and be frisked by an El Al guard before their plane took off for Paris and New York. Then I got into my chauffeured limousine and drove back to the city. It was Wednesday and my people were waiting. They needed me.